CHARLES WILLEFORD
WILD WIVES

"She wasn't wearing much beneath the skirt. In an instant it was all over. Fiercely and abruptly."

A classic of Hard-boiled fiction, Charles Willeford's *Wild Wives* is amoral, sexy, and brutal. Written in a sleazy San Francisco hotel in the early 1950's while on leave from the Army, Willeford creates a tale of deception featuring the crooked detective Jacob C. Blake and his nemesis—a beautiful, insane young woman who is the wife of a socially prominent San Francisco architect. Blake becomes entangled in a web of deceit, intrigue and multiple murders in this exciting period tale.

"No one writes a better crime novel."—Elmore Leonard

"Mr. Willeford never puts a foot wrong, and this is truly an entertainment to relish."—*The New Yorker*

"Wow! He gives you...the viewpoint of the most fascinating asocial trash."—Tony Hillerman

RE/SEARCH PUBLICATIONS
180 VARICK STREET, 10TH FL., NEW YORK, NY 10014

Publishers/Editors: Andrea Juno and V. Vale
Production Manager: Lisa London

ISBN 0-940642-29-8

Copyright © 1987 by Charles Willeford and RE/Search Publications
Introduction copyright © 1987 by V. Vale & Andrea Juno

BOOKSTORE DISTRIBUTION: Consortium, 1045 Westgate Drive, Suite 90, Saint Paul, MN 55114-1065. TOLL FREE: 1-800-283-3572. TEL: 612-221-9035. FAX: 612-221-0124

NON-BOOKSTORE DISTRIBUTION: Last Gasp, 777 Florida Street, San Francisco, CA 94110. TEL: 415-824-6636. FAX: 415-824-1836

U.K. DISTRIBUTION: Airlift, 26 Eden Grove, London N7 8EL. TEL: 071-607-5792. FAX: 071-607-6714

RE/SEARCH PUBLICATIONS, 180 Varick St, 10th Floor, New York, NY 10014-4606. TEL: 212-807-7300. FAX: 212-807-7355

Printed in Hong Kong by Colorcraft, Ltd
Cover Art by: Terri Groat-Ellner

CHARLES RAY WILLEFORD III:
PARTIAL BIOGRAPHY
(pseud. Will Charles)

1-2-1919	Born Little Rock, Ark., son of Charles Ray II and Aileen (Lowey) Willeford.
1936-1956	U.S. Army, retired as Master Sergeant. USA, Philippines, Europe, etc. Military Awards: Silver Star, Bronze Star, Purple Heart, Luxembourg Croix de Guerre.
7-1-1951	Married Mary Jo Norton, an English professor.
1956	Beacon Fiction award for *Pick-Up*.
1960	Palm Beach Jr. College: A.A.
1962	University of Miami, B.A. (magna cum laude)
1964	M.A. Associate editor, *Alfred Hitchcock Mystery Magazine*.
1964-1967	Coral Gables, Fla: University of Miami, instructor in humanities.
1967-1985	Miami, Fla: Miami-Dade Junior College, taught English and philosophy (asso. professor, etc).
1973	Mark Twain Award for *Cockfighter*.
1974	*Cockfighter* made into movie starring Warren Oates, etc.
10-1976	divorced
1987	*Miami Blues* optioned for movie.
Other:	[source: *Contemporary Authors*, New Revision Series, Vol. 15] Columnist for *Village Post, Miami Herald, Mystery Scene* (3840 Clark Rd SE, Cedar Rapids IA 52403, sample issue $6), articles in *Books Abroad, Saturday Review, Playboy, Writer's Digest, Sports Illustrated, Air Force, Publishers Weekly, Armchair Detective* (129 West 56th St, NYC 10019, sample issue $8). Biographical articles in *Harpers, The Face, Spin*, etc. Member: Authors League of America, Mystery Writers of America, Vorpal Blades. Quotation: "I had a hunch that madness was a predominant theme and a normal condition for Americans living in the second half of this century. The publication of *The Machine in Ward Eleven* (1963) and its reception by readers confirmed what I had only heretofore suspected."

BIBLIOGRAPHY

POETRY:

The Outcast Poets (1947) portfolio of Willeford & 4 other poets gathered in an envelope; #8 in the Alicat Book Shop Press "Outcast" Chapbook Series

Proletarian Laughter (1948) Alicat #12, 1000 copy press run

Poontang (1967) New Athenaeum Press, Crescent City, FL, 500 copy press run

NOVELS:

High Priest of California (1953), Royal Giant Editions pb; bound with Full Moon, a novel by Talbot Mundy

Pick-Up (1954), Beacon Book pb #109; repr. 1967 Softcover Library pb; repr. 1987 Black Lizard Books pb

Wild Wives (1956) Beacon Book pb, bound with *High Priest of California* (orig title of *Wild Wives: Until I Am Dead*)

Honey Gal (1957) Beacon Book pb (orig title: *The Black Mass of Brother Springer*)

Lust Is A Woman (1957) Beacon Book pb (orig title: *Made In Miami*) Reprinted 1967, Softcover Library pb

The Woman Chaser (1960) Newstand Library pb (orig title: *The Director*)

Understudy for Love (1961) Newstand Library pb

No Experience Necessary (1962) Newstand pb

The Burnt Orange Heresy (1971) Crown hb. Reprinted 1987 by Black Lizard Books.

The Hombre From Sonora (1971) Lenox Hill Press (Crown) hb under pseudonym "Will Charles" (orig title: *The Difference*). Reprinted 1973 by Robert Hale, London in hb.

Cockfighter (1972) Chicago Paperback House B-120. Reprinted 1974 as Avon pb. Reprinted 1987 by Black Lizard Books

Off the Wall (1980) Pegasus Rex Press, fictionalized hb biography of the "Son of Sam" (David Berkowitz)

Miami Blues (1984) St Martin's Press hb. Reprinted 1985 in Ballantine pb

New Hope For The Dead (1985) St Martin's Press hb

Sideswipe (1987) St Martin's Press hb

Kiss Your Ass Goodbye (Oct 1987) Dennis McMillan; signed & numbered edition of 400 copies

SHORT STORY COLLECTION:

The Machine in Ward Eleven (1963) Belmont pb; repr. 1964 by Consul Bks, U.K.

NON-FICTION:

A Guide for the Underhemmorrhoided (1977) privately printed, 1000 copies

Something About A Soldier (1986) Random House hb

I Was Looking for a Street (unpublished, ms completed)

Jim Tully: The Underworld Years (in preparation, a bio)

New Forms of Ugly (critical study of modern literature), Dennis McMillan Pubs

INTRODUCTION

America is rediscovering, on a massive scale, the cynical, hard-boiled novels of Jim Thompson, David Goodis, Charles Willeford, and others that were a product of the fifties/early sixties—the last transitional decade before television saturated language. At a time when millions of relatively ordinary folk still *read*, these books satisfied the universal craving for adventure, romance, psychological understanding and linguistic surprise, at their best providing a wealth of blunt street-*poetic* dialogue amidst sudden, unexpected acts and counter-acts.

While masculine and feminine characterizations were often ludicrously polarized, nevertheless a harsh, deeply realistic unsentimentality prevailed, occasionally veering toward dark, psychotic depths. The doomsday mentality engendered by the post-nuclear age Cold War lent an edge of despair to the ruthless greed and desire manifested by the power-hungry characters starring in these black thrillers. A type of hero without ideals, possibly even mentally unbalanced, was asserting itself. In contrast to the bland, homogenized speech and entertainment purveyed by today's mass media, this fiction was strong and colorful, etching vivid pictures in the reader's mind. The power of this language yet survives to speak to new generations of readers dissatisfied with the superficial, predictable quality of experience commonly accepted as adult entertainment.

Charles Willeford's 1953 first novel, *The High Priest of California*, offers a rare treat: the opportunity to see the world through the eyes of a ruthless, misogynistic near-psychopath, used-car salesman Russell Haxby, *without moral comment* on his acts. This radical approach is in direct counterpoint to most hard-boiled writers of the time. Usually such a character is presented from the out-side, with a pious commentary. Or the work will be propped up with some moral justification system, like a Mickey Spillane novel in which the hero, under the patina of "right"-ness, excuses nu-merous immoral and brutal acts in the defense of Manliness, God or Country.

By using the structure of a first-person narrative, Willeford makes the reader identify and empathize with the hero. Then repulsion intrudes when early on the author offers a stunning clue to the hero's nature: for no *good* reason he knees a parking attendant in the groin and judo-chops him to the ground, away from where his date can see. The first-person narration makes very little of it, yet this act of casual brutality is a shocker, an irrational act and a harbinger of more to come.

What makes *High Priest* exceptional is that here the hero's basic misogyny is *isolated*, undisguised by missions for patrio-tism, crime-solving or other reasons. The only mission in this book is to conquer a woman. Further, the hero's characterization is deep and complex—Russell Haxby, who listens to Bartok and tries to translate James Joyce's *Ulysses,* defies facile categorization as a villain. Even though his persona is pure hypocrisy and oppor-tunism (he's even willing to murder if he can get away with it), he also has far more wit, sardonicism and style than anyone else. And the first person narrative forces the reader to confront the character's unconscionable twists of evil lurking in one's own self.

In the hard-boiled tradition, Willeford's second 1953 novel, *Wild Wives,* stars Jake Blake, an amoral detective whose nemesis is the beautiful, insane young wife of a socially prominent, elderly San Francisco architect. Initially hired to shake off two goons who've been paid to follow her, Blake becomes entangled in a web of deception, intrigue and murder in which he ends up the fall guy. This work is completely contemporary in its homosexual characterizations and sexual morality, presenting some very col-orful players and scenarios.

Genuinely creative writing functions as *antidote* to the

mediocritizing language (mostly from television and newspapers) inundating us today. All of Charles Willeford's writing is marked by the unusual: devious plots, dialogue rich in innuendo, eccentric detailing of even the smallest roles, wry touches of perversity, sardonicism, plus an overall no-nonsense truth to character. Multiple levels of meaning and mystery, as well as authentic poetic inventiveness, are there to perform the vital function of renewing and refreshing our perceptions and reinvigorating our thought. Good writing, like the works reprinted here, can cut across time to find its own audience and assume new life on its own.

—V Vale and Andrea Juno, San Francisco, 1987

CHAPTER
1

The rain hit hard at my window. It slowed down to a whisper, then hit hard again. All afternoon the rain had been doing this while I sat behind my desk with my feet up, doing nothing. I looked around the ratty little office and wondered vaguely what time it was.

It wasn't much of an office. The four walls were painted a sickly lime-green, and the only bright spot in the room was the famous Marilyn Monroe calendar with its flame-red background. Two ladder-backed straight chairs, a two-drawer file cabinet, a cheap combination typing-and-writing desk and a swivel-chair completed the furnishings. The rugless floor was laid with brown and yellow linoleum blocks. As I sat facing the door, looking over my feet at the milk-glass pane, I could see in reverse the lettering of my name:

JACOB C. BLAKE
PRIVATE INVESTIGATIONS

Behind me was my single window with its excellent view of the air shaft. The office was on the mezzanine of the King Edward Hotel and it was probably the worst location for a private investigator in San Francisco. But I hung onto it for two reasons. One: I lived in the hotel. Two: It was cheap.

I lit a cigarette and tried my best to blow smoke rings. After several tries I blew a good one. While I watched it disintegrate the door opened and a girl entered. She was young and she held a pistol in her hand. I left my feet on the desk and raised my arms in the air as high as I could reach.

"Stick 'em up!" the girl said, out of the corner of her mouth.

"They are up." My voice came out higher than I'd ever heard it before. My body felt suddenly cold and damp. The girl came around to the side of my desk, shoved the pistol into my face and pulled the trigger. A jet of lukewarm water splashed on my forehead and dribbled into my eyes. The girl made a noise; a foolish, school-girl giggle.

My fear had become unreasoning anger. I jerked the black water pistol out of her hand and broke it in two. I threw the shattered plastic into the wastebasket, twisted my hands into the lapels of the girl's gabardine raincoat and started shaking her. I shook her so hard her head whipped back and forth like a marionette's. When she started to cry I cooled off. I shoved her into a chair and sat down again in my own. My hands were trembling from the combination of fear, anger, and now sudden remorse for ill-treating the girl. I took a calmer look at her.

She seemed about fifteen years old. A mop of auburn poodle-cut curls topped a pretty, innocent, delicate face. She carried a small, black patent-leather handbag and her shoes were single-strap Mary Janes. She took a tiny handkerchief out of her purse and dabbed at her blue eyes.

"You hurt me." Her voice was a bubbling, light soprano.

"You scared me."

"I was just having a little fun."

"It wasn't funny!"

She giggled. "You should have seen your face!"

"What were you trying to prove, anyway?" I smiled in spite of myself.

"I'm waiting for my brother," she explained.

"I see. You thought I was your brother."

"No! Freddy's visiting Mr Davis in his room and he told me to wait for him in the lobby."

"This is the mezzanine."

"I know that! But I've been waiting for over an hour, and

I've been exploring sort of, to kill time. I saw your office, and I wondered what a private detective would do if someone tried to stick him up, and then I remembered I had my little brother's water pistol with me—"

"The brother Freddy, visiting Mr Davis—"

"No! My *little* brother's water pistol! Freddy's my big brother. He's eighteen years old!"

"He won't let you use his water pistol?"

"My goodness! He doesn't even have one! That was my little brother's water pistol you broke up, and I'll have to get him a new one."

"What's his name?"

"Melvin. Melvin Allen."

"And what's your name?"

"Barbara Ann. They call me Bobby, but I hate it. Don't you?"

"Is your last name Allen too?"

"Of course it is, and my big brother Freddy, the one upstairs visiting Mr Davis—his name is Allen, too!"

"Then it isn't Freddy?"

"Yes! Freddy Allen."

"The one upstairs. The one who doesn't own a water pistol."

"That's right. My, you sure do have a hard time understanding things!"

"I think I'll give you a spanking." I was having a lot of fun with the girl. Barbara Ann had put some life into a dull, dreary day. Her eyes widened, and for a moment, she stared at me with a scared expression on her innocent face. Then the corners of her mouth turned up slightly and formed a knowing, truly feminine smile. Without a word she got up from her chair, removed her raincoat, folded it, and put it on the seat. She leaned well over the desk, reached behind her and lifted her plaid skirt, exposing pink panties and a firm, beautifully rounded bottom.

"Go ahead," she said calmly. "Spank me. I deserve it."

This was my second surprise of the afternoon. And I would have enjoyed giving a spanking to her. But my native intelligence came to my rescue. I reached over and pulled her skirt down, resisting my strong desire to pat her nicely rounded buttocks.

"I didn't *think* you'd do it," she said scornfully, tossing her curls. She put her raincoat back on.

"You knew I wouldn't do it," I said, "but you'd better watch out for that cute little rear end of yours. Next time, you might not be so lucky. And now, with that fatherly advice, you can leave. Beat it."

I put my feet back up on the desk. Barbara Ann pulled a chair up close and sat down. She was prim and business-like. Her hands were folded neatly in her lap and there was a set, serious glint in her blue eyes.

"Mr Blake," she began earnestly, "I proved something when I came in here with that toy pistol. I showed you how alert I was, and how nervy a younger girl can be. Why, no one would ever suspect a girl like me of being a private detective, and I could get away with almost anything."

"Go on."

"Well, I'm still going to high school, but I don't go on Saturdays, and I can stay out real late at night, and Daddy never says anything. Many times I come in as late as eleven o'clock and still he doesn't say anything. So how about giving me a part-time job working for you?" She sat back in the chair.

"How old are you, Barbara?"

"I'm going on sixteen, but I look a lot older."

"I can see how old you look." I shook my head. "That's too young. I'd lose my license. But even if you were older I couldn't give you a job, kid. I don't have enough business to keep myself busy."

"Oh, you don't have to pay me, Mr Blake! I'll work for the experience—"

"I'm sorry, Barbara. I can read your mind. You think that being a private detective is a glamorous, exciting job—well, it isn't. It's a boring, underpaid profession. Doors slammed in your face, creditors after you all the time; soliciting work from cheap loan outfits, and you end up nine times out of ten with the dirty end of the stick. You don't want any part of it."

"But I do! And I'm going to sit right here until you give me an assignment." She set her pretty lips in a tight line.

"All right." I owed her something for the dirty trick she had played on me with the water pistol. "I'll give you an assignment. Without pay, of course."

"I told you, I don't care about that!"

"Listen carefully, then." I made up a lie. "Do you know where the big 'E' department store is?"

"The Emporium? Of course."

"Well, tomorrow, Saturday, they're having a sale on women's ostrich-skin pocketbooks. These are very expensive, you know. Now, I've heard something through my sources in the underworld, which I can't divulge to anyone—you understand that?"

"Of course. You can't expose your stoolies."

"Right. There's a notorious shoplifter who's coming up from Los Angeles expressly for that one sale. My job is to get her. But, unfortunately, she knows me and that's where the trouble comes in. If she spots me, she won't steal any pocketbooks, and unless I can catch her red-handed, we can't prove anything. Do you follow me?"

"Oh, yes!" Barbara's eyes were round with excitement.

"But she doesn't know me and I can watch for her instead of you!"

"That's the idea. Here's what you do. I'll check with my sources tonight, and if she comes to town, I'll open my office door tomorrow morning and wave a handkerchief at exactly 8:30. If she doesn't come I won't open my door, and I can call you later if I find a suitable assignment. Okay?"

"I get it. I'll watch your office door from the lobby in the morning and if the shoplifter is in town you'll wave a handkerchief. Then what do I do?"

"Go down to the big 'E' and hang around the counter where the ostrich-skin handbags are. When you spot her lifting one, arrest her and turn her over to the manager.

"Aren't you going to be there?"

"I told you already. She knows me."

"What does she look like?"

"I don't know," I said truthfully. "I've never seen her."

"You can depend on me, Mr Blake. I won't let you down." Barbara stood up. I shook hands with her gravely.

"Until tomorrow then."

"Right. 8:30 sharp." She left the office, her cheeks glowing with excitement. I felt a slight tinge of remorse, but I shrugged it away. The hell with it. Do her good. At the time I didn't know that I was making a terrible mistake by playing a practical joke on Barbara Ann Allen. It seemed like an amusing idea, a way to get rid of the kid, but no man can see into the future, and even now, I have no regrets.

I smoked a cigarette with enjoyment. It's the little surprises in life that go to make a good day. When nothing ever happens, the day is a lousy one. My whole outlook was changed by Barbara's visit. I decided to do a little work. I cracked the telephone book to the yellow section to look up addresses of loan companies, intending to solicit a few skip-tracing jobs by correspondence . . . but again my door opened and I looked up.

No teenager this time. This was a woman. She was about twenty-six or -seven, with sparkling drops of rain dotting a thick mass of dark, almost blue-black hair. Her face was very pale. This made her eyes, which were the color of freshly washed blackberries, appear even darker than they were. She had plenty upstairs, but her posture was erect and her body slim, with narrow hips. She closed the door and stood with her back against it, smiling at me with a set of little white teeth. The teeth weren't perfect; they slanted toward the center lightly.

"Are you Mr Blake?" she asked, raising her dark eyebrows.

"Yes, I am. Won't you sit down?" I pointed to the chair

vacated by Barbara Ann.

She removed a slick raincoat, exposing a tailored suit of heavy ochre tweed. I could see the sticks and twigs in the material. It was at least a two-hundred-dollar suit.

She removed her yellow gloves and tossed them on the desk. She sat down and crossed her legs and we waited each other out.

"Do you know who I am?" she asked.

"Am I supposed to know? This is a good-sized city." I smiled.

"My name is Florence Weintraub." Her voice was flat, toneless.

"Yes?"

"My father is Milton Weintraub."

"I've heard of him. He's the architect who built those city projects."

"That's right. He's my father."

"And what can I do for you?"

"I'll show you. Open your door a crack and take a look around the lobby."

I got up, moved to the door, opened it and scanned the lobby. In addition to the lobby regulars and the easily spotted tourists, I saw two men who didn't belong there. Both were the bruiser type, big enough to wrestle for TV. One was standing by the entrance pretending to read a newspaper and the other was lolling near the short staircase leading to the mezzanine. As I watched they exchanged glances, and the man with the newspaper shrugged.

"See what I mean?" Miss Weintraub was at my shoulder and I got a whiff of the perfume in her hair.

"Yeah, I dig them." We backed into the office.

"Those two men are holding me prisoner."

"Why?" I didn't doubt it. They were rugged enough to do it.

"They've been hired by my father. They follow me everywhere I go; except the bathroom. In fact, they think I'm in the ladies' room now."

"I see. But you don't know why your father hired them?"

"Certainly I know," she said bitterly. "He's afraid I'll get into some kind of trouble. If I enter a bar they follow me in, take me by the arm and lead me outside again. If I start an innocent conversation with anybody, they get right on me, both of them. 'Oh, here you are, Florence!' they say, and off we go. After I've been removed from whoever it was I happened to talk to, they let me go again and fall in behind me. How would you like it?"

"I wouldn't like it, Miss Weintraub."

Her purplish eyes were angry and her breathing was quick. She was beautiful this way, very much so, and yet there was something about her that put me on my guard.

"How old are you, Miss Weintraub?"

"Twenty-six," she said without hesitating. "Certainly old enough to dispense with nursemaids."

"I agree. What do you want me to do? Lose them for you?

"Can you?"

"For a while. They can pick up your trail again easily enough. That can be done by returning to where they first lost you, or to your home, or by checking your regular hangouts—many ways. But if you want to lose them for an hour or so, it can be done."

"I'd like to lose them permanently."

"The only way to do that is have your father call them off. Want me to talk to him for you?"

"Oh, no! That wouldn't do any good."

"Without more thought on it, then, that's all I can suggest."

"Could we lose them for two hours, Mr Blake?"

"Sure."

She took a checkbook out of her purse, raised her eyebrows.

"Twenty-five bucks a day and expenses," I said, and I sat back, waiting for an argument.

She filled in a check and handed it to me. It was for fifty dollars. I folded the check, put it in my wallet and got to my feet. I opened the second drawer of my file cabinet and got my slicker and hat. I put them on.

"Have you a watch?" I asked. She nodded. "All right. Give me eight minutes, then walk through the lobby to the door, turn left up Powell, and when I come by in a cab, I'll whistle. Make for the cab on the run and well leave them stranded at the curb. Okay?"

"Eight minutes."

"Right."

I opened the door and closed it softly behind me.

CHAPTER
2

As I walked through the lobby, I took a better look at the two bruisers. The larger, standing by the staircase, had a face as roughly textured as a second-hand football. He wore a gray suit. The other man, while not as tall, was almost as wide through the shoulders as the back of a Greyhound bus. Someone had sold him a Harris tweed (ugh!) double-breasted suit.

I climbed into a cab at the hack stand on the corner and told the driver to go around the block. The traffic was heavy, and it took almost four minutes to complete the circuit. As I had suspected, Miss Weintraub was already outside and standing on the sidewalk. She looked nervously up and down the block. There isn't a woman in the world who can follow instructions and I'd counted on this fact when I had told her to wait eight minutes.

"Stop here," I told the driver. He slammed on the brakes and I whistled. Miss Weintraub ran blindly across the street, narrowly avoiding an up-dragging cable car, and got in beside me. I pulled the door shut.

"Drive down to Market," I instructed the driver, "and turn right to Van Ness. Take another right at Geary and when you hit the Union Square Garage, pull inside."

Miss Weintraub looked out of the window and bit her thumbnail. The hackie moved the heavy vehicle out with a jerk and I settled back in the seat.

"Relax," I told her. "We'll get rid of them."

"I've tried cabs before." She shook her head. "I think there's too much traffic to get away."

We were on Market Street, and I couldn't see anyone behind us. The driver barked over his shoulder: "I just thought of something. I can't make no left turn into the Union Square Garage. There's a sign."

"Don't worry about it," I said. "You make the turn anyway. It'll only take a minute and you can dodge out the other side. If you get a ticket, I'll take care of you."

"I'll try it—"

We turned right at Geary and the driver made good time to the Square. Ignoring the NO LEFT TURN sign he angled his wheels hard and skidded to a stop inside the garage. We got out of the cab and I handed him three bucks. I took Miss Weintraub by the arm and led her into the tunnel.

"Where does this go?"

"To the lobby of the Saint Francis," I said.

"I never knew this tunnel was here."

"I'm hoping your friends don't know about it either."

As soon as we gained the lavish lobby I took a short breather, reaching for a cigarette. Then I remembered they were still on my desk, and with the girl holding my arm, I headed for the cigar counter. The man in the gray suit was smoking a cigar and leaning against the counter. His leathery face wore a wide grin. He lifted the brim of his hat, pulled it down again.

"Oh, there you are, Miss Weintraub."

"Where's your friend?" I asked pleasantly, hiding my chagrin.

"He's outside waiting in the car, but we aren't taking you along. I'd like to, but it's a private party. Some other time, maybe."

He was cocky, well pleased with himself. Miss Weintraub's face was pale except for her cheeks. They had turned a mottled red. She gave me a helpless look, and that did it. I stretched my arms out; my left above my head, my right almost to my knee, and yawned as if I were bored. I brought my right fist up from my knee and caught the man in the belly, an inch above his belt buckle. His lungs were full of cigar smoke and the smoke belched out of his mouth with a loud whoof. His knees sagged and he dropped to the floor in a praying position.

"Let's go!" I said. We walked briskly through the lobby toward the Powell Street entrance, ignoring the looks passed our way. A cab was waiting in the white zone and the doorman opened the door for us. We climbed inside, and he closed the door.

"Golden Gate Park," I said. The driver bluffed his way into the traffic stream. "I still haven't got a cigarette."

"Here," Miss Weintraub said, taking a pack of Marlboros out of her purse. "Oh, that was simply wonderful! The look of surprise on his face was marvelous. I didn't expect you to hit him!"

"Neither did he."

When we reached the park I had the driver circle through the grounds for five minutes before I was satisfied no one was following us. It was almost dark and the rain was coming down as hard as ever.

"We've lost them," I said. "Where do you want to go now?"

"My car is parked in the lot at Eighth and Market."

"Do they know it?"

"I don't think so. I had some work done on it yesterday and I told the mechanic to park it there for me. I gave him a five dollar tip . . . "

"Drive to the parking lot at Eighth and Market," I told the driver. I leaned back on the seat and closed my eyes. Tomorrow I could expect two visitors. Perhaps I should wear my gun. The man in the gray suit surely would be looking for a little revenge for the belt in the belly. I sighed. Sometimes twenty-five bucks a day didn't seem to be enough money for what I had to go through to earn it. Then I smelled perfume. Soft lips covered mine and an arm curled around my neck. I opened my eyes. Miss Weintraub's firm, insistent tongue pried my teeth apart and I responded gallantly. The kiss lasted a long time. She was the first to break away, not me. She folded her hands self-consciously in her lap.

"That was for being so brave. And if that isn't good enough

for an excuse, I'll think of another."

"If you can't think of another one, ask me," I said.

We got her blue Roadmaster out of the parking lot and she drove through town to the cut-over for the Golden Gate Bridge.

"There's a place in Sausalito that you'll like, Jake." With only one kiss, we were now on a first-name relationship. "We can have dinner, and maybe dance afterward. I haven't been out in a long time."

"Suits me, Florence. After a day like today I could stand a drink and a steak."

I watched her as she drove. She was expert enough, although I thought she took too many chances darting in and out of traffic. She concentrated on what she was doing, however, and kept the big Roadmaster under perfect control. After we crossed the bridge we dropped down the narrow winding two-lane highway that led to Sausalito. When the road leveled she made a left turn up an unpaved cliff road, dropped to low-drive, and we twisted and turned for two miles before we reached the top of the cliff and swerved into a gravel parking lot. A blue neon sign flashed intermittently from the roof of a long, low red-brick building:

THE KNOCKOUT CLUB

"Ever been to this place, Jake?"

"I didn't know it was here. I don't have a car."

"You'll like it."

She parked as close to the building as she could and we dashed for it through the wet. I checked our raincoats and my hat while she went into the ladies' room. The bored headwaiter raised his chin and lowered his eyelids the way they do and I held up two fingers. He nodded and I got a pack of Camels out of the machine next to the checkroom. I smoked one and a half cigarettes while I waited for Florence. The wait was worth every minute of it. When she appeared, Florence had undergone a complete transformation. She looked as if she had spent the entire afternoon in a beauty parlor. Her fine dark hair was piled high on top of her head and held in place with two plain silver combs. She had added the faintest blush to her cheeks and colored her full lips a coral red.

We were early and there were only a few other couples on hand. The room was large, dark, and lighted solely by the electric candles on the occupied tables. I told the waiter to bring us two Martinis while we looked over the menu.

"You'll like the trio, Jake." Florence smiled. "They're nervous."

"Fine. I like nervous trios. What do you want to eat?"

"You order. Men are so much better at ordering than women are."

I ordered two rare sirloins and while we waited we drank our second Martini. She didn't ask for my olive and I liked her for this one non-feminine trait.

We didn't talk to each other, because we both had the same thing on our minds, and talking wasn't necessary. How long would we have, and would there be enough time to do what we wanted to do before her father's bodyguards caught up with us? After the kiss in the cab I could easily see why Milton Weintraub kept a guard on his daughter. She wasn't the type who is hard-to-get; she was *anxious*-to-get!

The steaks arrived, swimming in mushroom gravy, and with their appearance the curtain behind the ridiculously small dance floor swept upward and revealed the imprisoned trio on the raised stand. It was a colored trio consisting of guitar, accordion and bongo drums. They wore tuxedo trousers and red dinner jackets. White ties. They started off right with a mambo arrangement of *Tangerine,* and the bongo thumper did things with the beat that I didn't know were possible.

"Let's dance," I said, and I took a large bite of steak to hold me over for a while.

"Do you know what they call themselves?" We picked our way through the empty tables to the dance floor.

"No," I said, chewing.

"The Knockout Drops."

We started to dance. Florence was remarkably good. She clung to me like jello to a moulding tin, following my lead as though we'd practiced the mambo at Arthur Murray's for ten years. When the music stopped we walked over to the stand. The leader smiled widely and hit three questioning chords on his guitar.

"Please play, 'I Got It Bad—'"

"And that ain't good!" He finished for me.

"Play it." I opened my wallet. The smallest I had was a ten-dollar bill. I gave it to him. "Play it ten times."

"Yes, sir!" He slammed his foot down and they went into it. The first time through they played it slow, not sickening slow but danceable. After the third chorus some of the other dancers threw hard looks at the trio. The bongo bumper sang the fourth chorus and he was so good nobody minded the repetition of the song. Perfect enunciation, and yet you didn't exactly follow the words. Just the meaning. Before he finished the chorus I led Florence across the room to the side double-doors leading outside. We closed the doors behind us and we were standing on a narrow three-foot ledge that overlooked the parking lot. The night was inky black and it was still raining. We were partly protected by a striped awning, but now and then the wind would whip the rain in on us and it would get to our legs. Through the white-curtained double-door I could see a man and a woman eating at a table less than three feet away from us. This lent an extra excitement to my ardor, along with the knowledge that any car entering the parking lot with its lights on would pick us out against the building. I pulled Florence hard against me and kissed her.

"Here?" I asked.

"Oh, yes! Here! Now!"

I gathered the heavy tweed of her skirt in my fingers, and lifted. The heat of her body reached out for my hands. The flesh of her was firm and yet oddly relaxed. She wasn't wearing much beneath the skirt. In an instant it was all over. Fiercely and abruptly. Florence arranged herself, opened the door and walked across the dining room to the ladies' room. I had to light and take several drags on a cigarette before my hands stopped shaking enough for me to go back inside. When I did go in the man eating by the door looked at my face and gave me a wide grin. I wiped my face and mouth with my handkerchief and got rid of the lipstick.

The trio was still playing "I Got It Bad." I laughed out loud on my way to the men's room. Florence would hardly be satisfied with the rapidity of my attack; we'd have to do better than that . . .

Florence still hadn't returned to our table when I got back from the men's room, so I crossed to the trio stand and talked with the leader.

"That was real low down," I complimented him. "Very nice."

"That's the way we play it," he said seriously. "We're specialists. Real spelunkers. All the way down!" He grinned happily.

"Play it ten more times." I took a ten-dollar bill out of my wallet.

"Man, I can't do it," he said, shaking his head from side to side, his eyes on the bill in my hand. "You want me to get fired?"

"Okay. Take it anyway."

"Thank you, sir!" He examined the bill into his pocket.

Florence still hadn't returned, but I started in on my steak. It was cold, but it tasted wonderful. Florence appeared, and I held her chair for her. Her eyes were very bright.

"Our two hours are up," she said unhappily.

"Don't worry about it. Eat your steak. You'll need it."

CHAPTER
3

After we finished our beef I ordered two B&B's, bypassing the dessert. Florence got moody on me and smoked a Marlboro in an ivory holder, sulking like a young girl deprived unjustly of her weekly allowance. I took my notebook out of my breast pocket and added up the expenses. When I finished my figuring, I grinned at Florence across the table.

"The fifty you gave me won't cover the expenses. Counting tips to the band, you owe me another twenty for today's work."

"Do I get any credit for the assistance I gave you on the porch?" She jerked her head toward the window.

"I'm not charging you for that," I said solemnly.

Florence's head tilted back and she laughed heartily, with her mouth open. "You drive a hard bargain, Jake Blake, but I've had a good time. When do we do this again?"

"It's up to you."

"I've got to go home now. Daddy'll be angry if I don't get in early. But if I go home as though nothing has happened, and don't admit that I purposely evaded the guards, I'm sure they won't tell him they lost me for the evening. He pays them well, you see. In a way, we play a kind of game—grown-up hide-and-seek. I'm sick of it, but I've been going along with it for several weeks."

"What, exactly, did you do to make father put a bodyguard on you?"

"You wouldn't believe me if I told you."

"I might and then I might not."

"Do you have to know?"

"No, I don't have to know."

"Then let's skip it. We'd better go."

I paid and tipped the waiter, redeemed our coats at the checkroom and we left the club. The rain had stopped and a smoke-thick fog had taken its place. Florence eased the car down the steep cliff road in low-drive. When we reached Highway 101 she opened the vehicle up and we crossed the Golden Gate Bridge at eighty miles an hour. This type of speed on a foggy night made me a trifle nervous, but I didn't say anything. It was her car, and if she wanted to wreck it, the hell with her.

"Where do you live, Jake?"

"Room 720 at the King Edward."

"That's nice. You can ride the elevator down to work."

"True. That's one of the reasons I took the mezzanine office. But it's a lousy location. I rarely have any walk-in business. There's not much I can do about it now, though. I signed a two-year lease."

"And you don't have a car?"

"I don't need one. It's easier to ride a cab or cable car. A car's a nuisance in San Francisco."

"You keep the Buick then. If you're going to work for me, and you seem to think it's work, you'll need a car. I'll drive home and I'll call you as soon as I get an opportunity."

"All right, I'll keep the car, but you'll have to pay for the gas and oil."

Her laugh wasn't so free and easy this time. "Don't carry this expense thing too far, Jake."

"You're the one who put it on a business basis. If you want to work things out my way, all you have to do is say so."

"What's your way?"

"Let me talk to your old man. After all, this is a ridiculous situation. Bodyguards, home by ten, sneaking around—"

"We'll do it my way, Jake. Don't go near my father! Do you understand?"

"I won't. Don't get excited."

We rode in silence the rest of the way. Florence lived in the old Nob Hill section of the city in a venerable house set well back from the street. The grounds surrounding the house still contained grass, trees and gravel paths. This was a bit unusual for this section of the city. The other houses in the same neighborhood were jammed against each other. She parked at the curb instead of taking the sweeping driveway leading into the deep front lawn and fronting the entrance to the house.

"I'll walk from here," she said. "You take the car and I'll call you some time tomorrow and tell you where to meet me."

"Fine. Just call the hotel. My phone's on an extension from the switchboard. It saves paying a telephone answering service—"

"Do you always think of money?"

"Only when I don't have any."

"From now on, lover boy, money will be the least of your worries."

She pushed my hat off my head, put her arms around my neck and kissed me. I felt the blood stir in me where it felt the most sensitive. I did my own kissing after that. I clutched Florence by the hair and pulled her head and face in tight against mine. She pulled away from me.

"No, Jake," she said hoarsely. "Not here in front of the house. I'll call you in the morning, just as soon as I can." She opened the door and got out of the car. I scrunched across the nylon seat covers to the driver's side and pushed the button that slid the window down.

"Goodnight," I said.

"Goodnight," she whispered. She ran through the open gate and up the graveled path. I was out of breath. I felt as if I had been running. I shoved the dash-lighter in and took a cigarette out of my pack. The lighter clicked out and the car door jerked open at the same time. A hand clutched the collar of my raincoat and another caught my left wrist and twisted it up behind my back as I was dragged out of the car. I tried to break away, but the hand that held my collar had shifted to my neck. Two thick fingers were jabbed deep into my throat. With a sudden movement I jerked forward and the sharp pressure on my twisted arm caused me to yell out. A hard wrist now held me under the throat and if I remained as still as possible I was merely in agony. Any movement at all was more painful than I could possibly bear. Through a film I could see the tall man in the gray suit standing in front of me with a wide grin on his face. That meant that Double-breasted was the one holding me. The tall man was talking and I did the best I could to listen.

"I told you it was a private party, Mr Blake, but you wouldn't listen to me." His voice was very pleasant, like a waiter recommending pressed duck. "You mustn't butt in when you're not invited."

He drew his fist back. I saw it coming but I didn't feel it. It was a sure-shot solar plexus blow and the film turned a dirty black, interspersed with shooting stars . . .

There was a drip-drop, drip-drop sound. The back of my head was wet and my first thought was that I was lying in a pool of blood. I sat up and blinked my eyes several times to get them in focus. I was on a well-kept lawn under an apple tree. The dripping noise was the water dribbling through the leaves of the tree and dropping into several shallow pools. My head had been in one of them. It was raining again, and hard, but under the tree it only filtered through. My hat was out in the rain, partially filled with water. I got to my feet and instantly bent double again with the pain in my stomach. I straightened up slowly, retrieved my hat and dumped the water out of it. I could see the outline of Florence's house through the other trees. There was a light in one of the upstairs windows. The rest of the house was dark. Bending over slightly to ease the pain in the pit of my stomach I staggered across the grounds to the wrought iron gate.

The Buick was gone.

I stumbled down the hill for five blocks before I hit a street with traffic. Sitting on a fire hydrant, I waited for ten minutes before a cab came along. On the ride to my hotel I seriously considered dropping the business with Florence Weintraub. But there was money to be made out of the screwy situation, I figured. Maybe a whole lot of money, and besides, Florence had something that I'd never run into before in my entire life. During the many years I had spent in the army, I'd met women in Paris, Berlin, Manila and Tokyo, but never, never one like her before. The mundane domestic variety I'd clashed with in the States I didn't count at all—I decided to stick it out for awhile to see what would happen.

Certainly I was more clever than the two men who had worked me over . . . I ought to be able to protect myself from such.

But why had her father hired them, anyway? My mind was too foggy to think. When I got to my room I undressed and got under the shower. I let the hot water beat down on my head and body until I relaxed enough to sprawl across my bed and go to sleep.

CHAPTER
4

I awoke the next morning at six; a nasty habit carried over from the army and one that I couldn't break. I was very sore. There was a large blue bruise on my stomach and two more bruises on my left side. I must have been kicked in the ribs after I had lost consciousness. I showered, shaved and dressed hurriedly. I detested the ascetic bareness of my hotel room. Although I'd lived in Room 720 for more than a year, I had added nothing of my own to its bareness. It was merely an ordinary hotel room, furnished with the minimum, ordinary furnishings familiar to guests of all second-rate hotels. It was still a place meant for transients. My suitcase, the suits hanging in the closet, and the fresh laundry in a brown-paper package on the dresser were the only evidences of my occupancy.

Every drawer except the bottom drawer of the dresser was empty. It was my practice to keep my dirty laundry in the bottom drawer, and to use my clean laundry from my returned bundle as I needed it. I kept the fresh bundle on top of the dresser; partly to see how I stood on clean laundry and partly to cover up the lower part of the mirror, which was distorted by ripples.

Carrying my hat and raincoat, I rode the self-operated elevator down to the mezzanine and entered my office. I put the slicker and hat into the empty file drawer, ordered my usual breakfast on the extension phone, and lit my first cigarette of the day. I smoked two before my breakfast arrived.

Old Timmy, the ancient bellboy, entered the office and put the tray on my desk.

"Thanks, Timmy. Put it on the bill."

"Yes, sir, Mr Blake." He hesitated.

"That's all."

"Yes, sir. This isn't me, Mr Blake. This is the man, but he said your bill is mighty high to keep on ordering meals without paying what you owes already . . . " He trailed off nervously.

"Who said that?"

"Mr Saunders in the coffee shop—"

"I'll tell you what to tell Mr Saunders," I said angrily. "You tell him that I don't want him to discuss my bills with the help. Do you understand that?"

"Yes, sir, Mr Blake."

"If he's got anything to say, he can say it to me! Now get the hell out of here."

"Yes, sir. I sure will tell him. I sure will." He sidled out, gently closing the door behind him.

My breakfast consisted of a double-shot of gin, a glass of orange juice and a pot of black coffee. I drank some of the orange juice, poured the gin in the space I'd made, and finished the glass. By the time I'd finished my coffee, the pains in my stomach and side were gone. I didn't feel like sitting behind my desk. I left the office and ran down the short flight of stairs to the lobby. I bought a newspaper at the cigar stand and turned to Earl Wilson's column. E.J. Stewart, the desk clerk, poked me in the shoulder with his forefinger and said:

"Do you know Mr Davis, Mr Blake? Jefferson Davis?"

"Not personally. He was a little before my time, E.J."

This E.J. Stewart was the oldest of the three desk clerks, and the friendliest, although I was on good enough terms with all three of them. Actually, none of them was named E.J. Stewart, but there was a beautifully carved, ornate, walnut nameplate on the desk labeled "E.J. Stewart," who long since had gone. It was too nice to throw away and none of the clerks had their own nameplates so, as a consequence, all of them were called "E.J." or "Mr Stewart" when they were on duty.

"No," the old man said nervously, "not that Jefferson Davis.

31

I mean Mr Davis, the art dealer; the man who lives here in the hotel in 624."

"I don't know him either. Did you read Earl Wilson this—"

"That's him over there." He pointed rather guardedly to an overstuffed couch where a man in gray spats and an Oxford gray suit sat reading a copy of *Art Digest*. His necktie was a blue-and-red paisley, and a black homburg was pushed well back from his forehead and partly covered steel-gray hair badly in need of cutting. He looked dignified despite the horsy length of his face and his outcropping of buck teeth.

"Yeah, E.J. I've seen him around the lobby several times, but I don't know him. What about it?"

"He said he wanted to meet you."

"I'm in my office all day. Why doesn't he come in, then?"

"He mentioned it casually the other day when he got his key. That's all I know."

I folded the newspaper, put it under my arm and walked over to the overstuffed couch.

"Mr Davis?" I asked politely.

He nodded, closed his magazine and got to his feet. "You're the detective chap, and I've been intending to visit you," he said. His upper teeth were well exposed when he smiled. "You are Mr Blake, are you not?"

"That's right. Can I help you in any way?"

"Well, no, not exactly." He laughed pleasantly. "I thought I might be able to help you. I reside in this dismal hotel myself, for the security, you know, and I understand that you too are a permanent resident."

"Yes. Unfortunately."

"I have an art gallery on Polk Street. Do you know where it is, Mr Blake?"

"Not exactly. But I've seen it. I'm aware of it."

"Well, my room here was pretty much the way yours is now—that is, if you haven't had your room decorated?"

"I haven't."

"I have, you see. It's completely changed, and I've put my entire collection of Paul Klees on the walls. Makes a difference. I thought you might like to see it some time with a view to doing something with your room to make it more attractive."

"I don't spend much time in my room, Mr Davis. And I certainly can't afford any Paul Klee art."

"Prints aren't so awfully expensive, and Klee isn't the only painter—he is for me, but I sell other things too. And whether you're interested or not, drop in some evening, have a drink, take a look at my collection. Tonight, perhaps."

"What do you want to see me about?" I asked him bluntly.

He colored slightly. "It's rather delicate . . . "

"All right, Mr Davis." I stuck my hand out and we shook hands. "I'll drop in this evening. I'd like to see your collection."

I returned to the desk and looked in my box. The mail wasn't in yet. I opened my newspaper to the sports page and E.J. poked me in the shoulder.

"What did you think of him?" He displayed great interest.

"Seemed like a nice old fellow. Why?"

"He's as gay as a bird dog!" The clerk laughed in a dirty way. "As gay as a bird dog!" He turned to answer the ringing telephone and I left the desk. As I walked across the lobby toward the staircase I looked sideways at Mr Davis. The clerk was merely guessing, I thought. Davis certainly didn't talk or act like the gay type to me. I climbed the stairs and entered my office where I could read my newspaper without interruption.

After I finished the paper I threw it into the wastebasket. As I sat idly behind my desk I suddenly remembered Barbara Ann. It was 8:27. I opened the door slightly and took a peek into the lobby. Barbara Ann was standing just inside the entrance and staring at my door. She was wearing dark glasses and a heavy, dark-brown overcoat. Her head was covered with a black beret. For a second I considered getting her upstairs and calling off the joke, but I knew she would only pester me for something else to do, and I didn't want to bother with her. I waved my handkerchief two or three times from the doorway and she turned abruptly and scuttled through the door like a woman rushing to a sale. I wondered vaguely if there were such things as ostrich-skin handbags. I knew there were wallets made out of ostrich skin, but I couldn't remember seeing women's handbags made out of the expensive leather. I shrugged and sat down behind my desk.

At nine, old Timmy brought my mail in, and put it on my desk.

"Did you tell Mr Saunders what I told you, Timmy?"

"Yes, sir, Mr Blake, I told him."

"What did he say?"

"He didn't say nothing, Mr Blake. Nothing at all."

"It's a good thing he didn't."

"Yes, sir, Mr Blake. It sure is a good thing." He left the office.

There was a letter from a woman in Mill Valley asking me how much I charged for handling divorce cases. I answered her letter with a postcard telling her I didn't handle divorce cases. If her husband happened to get the mail before she did, there would be an interesting argument between them, I speculated. There were two bills; one for a scarf I'd charged at the May Company, and another from Saul Bennet, the tailor. Bennet's had a rather bitter note attached, requesting at least a partial payment on the last suit I'd had made. I endorsed the fifty-dollar check Florence had given me and put it in an envelope which I addressed to Saul Bennet. I mailed the letter and postcard at the mail chute and returned to my office.

I waited until noon, and still no call from Florence. After deliberating whether to call her instead, I thought better of it and went out for lunch. I ate the special hot roast beef sandwich at Moar's cafeteria and returned to the hotel. When I opened my office door, Barbara Ann got up from the chair she was sitting on, flew across the room and did her best to claw me with her fingernails. I caught her wrists in time and held onto them, turning sideways to avoid being hit in the crotch by her pumping knee.

"Hold on," I said to her. "What's the idea?" I was holding her so that she couldn't do anything, but it didn't prevent her from spitting in my face until she ran out of saliva. I shoved her roughly into a chair and wiped my face with my handkerchief.

"You liar, you!" she shrilled at me. "You big, big, big, big fibber, you!"

"What's the matter? What are you talking about?"

"Ostrich-skin handbags!" she shouted. "That's what I'm talking about! There isn't any such thing at the Emporium. I looked all over the store. Everywhere. Finally, I talked to the assistant manager, and he told me he'd never heard of ostrich-skin handbags. You made it all up just to get even with me for shooting you with the water pistol. Didn't you? And there probably isn't any shoplifter, either!"

"What store did you go to, anyway?"

"The big 'E.' Just like you said."

"I didn't say the big 'E', I said the May Company. You're confused, that's what's the matter with you. You've failed me on your first assignment. The shoplifter's come and gone by now . . . "

"You did so say the big 'E'!" I could detect the small doubt in her voice. I pressed my advantage.

"No, I couldn't have told you that." I shook my head sadly. "The May Company is where the sale is, so why would I tell you the Emporium?"

"I don't know, but that's what you said."

"No, Barbara, I didn't. You made a mistake and then you try to blame it on me. I suppose now I'll have to do the job myself, as I should have done in the first place."

"I'm sorry, Mr Blake," Barbara said contritely. "Really I am, but I've got an awful temper and—"

"You'll never make a detective if you can't control your emotions any better than that. I'll give you one more chance. Go on over to the May Company and look through the store. You might catch the shoplifter stealing something else. Maybe it wasn't ostrich-skin handbags after all. Maybe it was plastic handbags—"

"They're too cheap to steal."

"You might be right. My stoolies may have been wrong. But go ahead and see what gives at the May Company. I'm giving you another chance."

"Yes, sir," she said happily. Barbara got up from the chair and kissed me. I pushed her away from me.

"Where did you learn to kiss like that?"

"We girls practice kissing at school sometimes. Why? Don't you like it?" She smiled mischievously.

"Beat it." She left the office, first putting her dark glasses over her eyes. Whew! I sat down behind my desk and lit a cigarette.

At 2:30 I had a telephone call. It was Florence.

"Did you think I wasn't going to call, Jake?"

"I was beginning to wonder."

"Can you pick me up at the Paramount Theatre on Market at six?"

"I haven't got your car anymore. Your two impetuous friends caught me with it last night and worked me over."

"They did?"

"They did."

"Where's the car now?"

"I don't know."

"Are you hurt bad?"

"Not that bad."

"Oh. Well, how about the Seal House, at the beach. I'll get away somehow and meet you there for dinner at six."

"Fine." She racked her phone.

There was no reason to hang around the office any longer. I had only waited for her telephone call. I took my hat and raincoat out of the file cabinet and put them on. The door opened and Florence's two bodyguards walked in.

"Going somewhere, Mr Blake?" The tall man asked the question. He was wearing blue serge instead of gray today. Double-breasted was still wearing his double-breasted. However, there was a pistol in his right hand. A large one. He handled it carelessly, pointing it in the general direction of my stomach. He smiled out of the side of his mouth.

"No. I wasn't going any place in particular," I said.

"Then we'll take you with us, if you don't mind. Mr Weintraub wants to talk to you. He wasn't happy about Florence going out to dinner with you last night, Blake."

"And I didn't like it either." Double-breasted put in his two cents.

"What are you going to do with that automatic?" I asked. "Shoot me, for Christ's sake?"

"Oh, no, nothing like that," the tall man said. "Would we, Melvin?"

Melvin shook his head. He was the one in the double-breasted.

"He didn't say to shoot him. He said to bring him in."

"Come on, Blake," the tall man said, all business now, "let's go. And don't try anything. Melvin wouldn't want to shoot you, but sometimes he gets nervous."

I preceded them out of the office and down the stairs. There was something odd about this. Weintraub must place a high value on his daughter to guard her into her twenty-sixth year. I walked slowly across the lobby trying to think of a way to get out of going along with the two gorillas. After all, there are limits to how many times a man should be worked over for one mistake. I didn't relish the prospect of another beating—I looked toward the entrance and a brief happy laugh escaped me. An old acquaintance of mine was coming through the door.

Detective Sergeant Ernest Tone.

CHAPTER
5

Sergeant Tone stopped inside the doorway, looked us over, and rubbed his chin with his left hand. After he eyed Melvin and the tall man suspiciously, he looked at me.

"What are you doing with these two creeps, Blake?"

"I was walking them to the door. I wanted to make sure they didn't steal anything on their way out."

"When did you get out, Ferguson?" Sergeant Tone asked the tall man.

"I've never been in, and you know it," Ferguson said defensively.

"When are you getting in, then?"

"I'm not. Let's go, Melvin." Ferguson and Melvin hurried out of the lobby and I remained with Tone. He was a little guy, not much more than 5'5", but he was a tough policeman. He rubbed his chin, cocked his head to the right like a bird.

"They wanted you for something, Blake. Something was up, and I could smell it."

"They were taking me somewhere to work me over, I believe. And then you appeared and they changed their mind."

"I'd like to pick them up—"

"Melvin's got a gun on him. Is that a reason?"

"I wish it was, Blake, but it ain't. He's got a license for it."

"That hood's got a license?"

"That's right, and don't ask me how he got it."

"Okay. What are you doing at the King Edward? Slumming?"

"In a way. I'm taking you in." Tone grinned.

"What for?"

"Ever heard of the Child Labor Act?"

"Yeah, what about it?"

"Come on." I followed him outside. A uniformed cop was sitting at the wheel of a police car by the curb and we climbed into the back seat. I was puzzled, but it was useless to pry any information out of Tone. If he wanted to tell me, he would; if not—and that was more likely—I could wait until we reached headquarters. I settled back comfortably in the seat.

"What's the story, Blake, on Melvin and Ferguson?"

"It's a case I'm on. Nothing confidential, I suppose. I'm working for Florence Weintraub—"

"Don't tell me you're mixed up with her!"

"Do you know the girl?"

"No, thank God!"

"Why? What's the matter with her?"

"Don't you know?"

"Well, I—"

"Everybody else does," he said grimly and tightened his thin lips.

"I've got an idea, maybe, but business is lousy, Tone. I need the dough."

"That's your concern. I'm not giving advice to private investigators. Right now, you'd better worry about your license, anyway."

"What's this all about, for Christ's sake?"

"I'll let Lieutenant Pulaski tell you about it. He thinks he's got your license this time, Blake. And maybe he has."

Nothing more was said. At the station we ducked under the stairs, entered the basement and walked down the hollow-sounding corridor to Lieutenant Stanley Pulaski's office. Pulaski was the Number Three man on the detective force, and was gradually working his way up to the Number One spot. He didn't like me very much. The newspapers had given me the credit instead of him on an attempted kidnap case about eight months before. I had done the go-between work and deserved the credit, but he didn't think so. Some people are that way . . .

Pulaski grinned at me when we entered his office. He was more than a little paunchy and liked to sit behind a desk. His desk was covered with various objects with which he fiddled as he talked. There was an ivory paperweight carved into the shape of a lion. There was an old-fashioned pen-and-ink stand in brass, with a container of sand, which he used instead of blotting paper. And there were several pictures of his wife and five children, each framed in heavy leather, and lined up across the desk like football linemen. The dark walnut desk was oversized, but Pulaski was large enough himself to overpower it and the many ornaments. His dew-lapped, blotchy face was happy as he pointed to a chair.

"Sit down, Blake," he said cordially. "I've been expecting you."

I sat down in the indicated chair. Sergeant Tone leaned against the wall and concentrated on stripping a wooden match into splinters. Slowly, maddeningly slow, Pulaski took a cigar out of his desk drawer and removed it from its glass tube. He sniffed the cigar with enjoyment, rolled it back and forth between his enormous hands, then very carefully cut the end off with a pair of tiny scissors. He lighted the cigar with a kitchen match, rolling it around in his mouth to insure an even light. He inhaled deeply, expelled the smoke with sensual satisfaction.

"Your business hasn't been too good lately, has it, Blake?"

"So-so," I said.

"More business than you can handle by yourself?"

"No. Not that much."

"Then why did you hire a teen-aged girl to work for you?" He shot this question angrily and the blotches on his face joined forces, making his face completely red.

"I didn't," I replied calmly.

"Bring her in, Tone," Pulaski ordered sharply. Sergeant Tone left the office and returned in less than a minute with Barbara Ann Allen. She was still wearing her brown coat and beret, but she had taken off her dark glasses. She was visibly frightened.

"All right, dear," the lieutenant croaked pleasantly, "tell us again about your assignment."

"Yes, sir." Barbara Ann looked to me for encouragement, but I kept a deadpan. "Mr Blake hired me, without pay—just for the experience, he said—to watch for a shoplifter in the May Company. Well, I didn't know exactly what department to look for her in and I didn't know what she looked like, but I thought to myself that the best place to look was where there were little things around that a woman could put in her purse or coat pocket. So . . . " She hesitated.

"Go on, dear," the lieutenant encouraged her.

"I've told you this before."

"Please tell it once more."

"Well, first I looked in the book department. I don't know why, but books are small, and people might want to steal a book, and there were a lot of people in that section of the store. I was standing by the counter where they sign people up for the Book-of-the-Month Club and I saw this woman slip a copy of *The Robe* under her coat. She pushed it up under her arm-inside her coat, and I could tell she was stealing it because it wasn't wrapped. So I grabbed her around the neck and called for help. The floorwalker came running over and I told him I saw her take the book. The woman was screaming like everything, but the floorwalker acted real nice and polite and took both of us into the little office in the back. I told him again that I saw her take the book. The woman said she didn't steal it. She claimed she was looking for a salesgirl. It was a lie, but when she paid for the book they let her go. But he kept me there and called the police . . . " Barbara Ann was almost in tears, but she shook her head and bravely continued. "I told you already that I was hired by Mr Blake, and you've kept me here ever since. I was just doing my duty and you're trying to make it look like I'm the one who's in the wrong!" She turned to me.

"Tell them to let me go, Mr Blake!"

"Well, Blake," the lieutenant said pleasantly, "what about it? Shall we turn your operative loose?"

I grinned. "What are you trying to pull, Lieutenant? I've never seen this girl before in my life."

Barbara Ann's eyebrows raised with amazement. "Why, you liar, you! You great big fibber, you! You did so tell me to go to May's and look for a shoplifter!"

"Not only do I don't know what you and the lieutenant are trying to pull," I said, "but I don't even know what you're talking about."

Barbara Ann made for me with her fists clenched. Sergeant Tone reached out quickly and caught her by the wrist.

"Take it easy, kid," he said quietly.

"You're lying, Blake," the lieutenant said. "A story like Barbara's can't be made up successfully, and you know it. It's screwy enough to be the truth."

"Okay," I said, shrugging, "charge me with it. See how far you get."

Pulaski thought it over. He looked sharply at Tone and Tone shook his head and shrugged. Holding his cigar like a dagger, Pulaski smashed it out in the ashtray on his desk.

"All right, Tone," he said, "get 'em out of here! Drive the girl home. You're a rotten bastard, Blake! I can't figure out what your purpose was, but I do know it was a cheap trick. I'd like to kick your teeth in!"

"Go ahead and hit me, Lieutenant," I said quietly. "I'll have you suspended."

Sergeant Tone opened the door for Barbara Ann, but she didn't budge. She stood motionless, both feet planted, still staring at me with amazement and anger.

"You'd better keep away from this man, Barbara," Pulaski told her with a kindness in his tone that was surprising. "We'll take care of him for you. Go on with the sergeant."

Tone and Barbara Ann left the office. I stood up, fished a cigarette out of my package and lighted it with one of the kitchen matches on the detective's desk.

"You're going to have to dream up a better frame than that to get my license, Pulaski," I said, putting as much disgust into my voice as I could under the circumstances. "You aren't even trying hard."

I left the office, slamming the door on my way out.

Sergeant Tone was leaning against the guardrail outside, puffing on a handmade brown cigarette. He raised his chin as I climbed the stairs and reached the sidewalk.

"What is the story, Blake?" he asked, hooking his short arms over the railing.

"There is no story," I replied. "Where's Bobby?"

"I sent her home in a police car. How did you know her name was Bobby if you've never seen her before?"

I laughed. "She's a teenager isn't she? Bobby-soxer? Bobby is short for bobby soxer."

"Pulaski wants your license pretty bad, Blake. I've got a hunch he's going to get it one of these days." Tone threw his cigarette into the street, turned away from me and ducked down the stairs into the basement.

At the next corner I caught a cab for the hotel.

CHAPTER
6

I rode the elevator up to my room, removed my clothes and got under a shower as hot as I could stand it. A visit to a police station makes me feel dirty all over. After I looked at my face in the bathroom mirror I decided I could get by without shaving again. I dressed carefully, selecting a shirt with a Mister "B" collar, and my one-button-roll, blue gabardine suit. I pulled on a pair of white clock sox and my gray suede shoes. It was hard to select a necktie. My wine-colored bow didn't look so good so I exchanged it for a cream-colored knitted tie. More contrast. I looked in the mirror admiringly for quite awhile. I really looked sharp.

As I started out of the room, the telephone rang. It was Jefferson Davis.

"My, I'm glad to catch you in, Mr Blake," he said. "I thought you might like to come down for a drink."

"What time is it now?"

"Oh, a little after four."

"What's your room number?"

"Six-twenty-four."

"All right, I'll be right down. I want to see those Klee paintings." I hung up.

Without waiting for the elevator, I took the corner stairway down one flight to the sixth floor. It was quicker. I knocked on the door and it opened immediately, as though Davis had been standing inside with his hand on the knob.

"What can I fix you, Mr Blake?" he asked pleasantly.

"Something with gin in it," I gulped. I could hardly talk.

The sight of his room had done something to my voice. It was a riotous blaze of varied color. His room was no longer than mine, but it seemed so; it did not have my dull, cocoa walls. Every available space contained a picture by Paul Klee, either an original or a print. It was similar to being caught up in the midst of a child's nightmare. The colors were breathlessly hot.

The room was furnished with new, modern furniture, and instead of a large double bed there was a two-seat, hide-a-bed sofa pushed up against the wall. It helped make the room look larger than mine, but the pictures closed the gap by appearing to leap out from the walls. Davis was fixing drinks on the coffee table and there was an amused smile on his face.

"How do you like them?" he asked, handing me a glass of orange juice and gin. He wore a wine-colored smoking jacket, gray slacks and red leather slippers. Somehow, without a hat, his long grayish hair looked natural. To cut it would have been a shame—in this exotic setting.

"Frankly, Mr Davis, I've never seen anything like it before. You said you had a few Klee's, but I didn't expect to see a room covered with them."

"He's my favorite painter," he replied, sipping his drink.

"He must be." I tasted mine. Cold and good.

"Sit down, sit down, Mr Blake." Davis graciously waved me to the sofa. I sat down, looking at the walls with my mouth partly open. The pictures must have cost him a fortune.

"What did you want to see me about?"

"Well, I didn't ask you here just to look at my art, I admit. . ." He sat beside me on the sofa, although there was a comfortable armchair directly across from me.

"Get to the point, Mr Davis. I can't stay too long."

"Now, now, don't rush me." He put his hand on my knee and squeezed gently. "You must spend the night with me sometime, Mr Blake." He smiled horsily.

"I've got my own room, Davis." I laughed. "And I'm too old for that sort of thing. I'm in my thirties. What you need"—I laughed again, and poured more gin into my glass—"is a young-ster."

Davis' smile was a trifle annoyed. "That's the crux of my problem, Mr Blake. I've got a youngster and I'm trying to get rid of him. I haven't actually thought things out yet—but, I suppose, that's one of the reasons I wanted to cultivate your friendship."

"We don't have to be friends," I grinned. "I charge twenty-five bucks a day and expenses."

"You wouldn't be interested in . . . "

"No. But I might be able to help you, after I find out what you want to do. I'm smarter than I look. I know, for instance, that your young boyfriend is Freddy Allen." I let that sink in. I had remembered Barbara Ann telling me she was waiting for her brother who was visiting Mr Davis.

Davis was startled. "Don't tell me we've been that obvious?"

"How old is Freddy now?" I asked the question casually, as though I knew Freddy Allen well, but couldn't remember his age.

"Twenty," he lied. "And I have no control over him whatsoever." He sighed. "You know Freddy, then?"

"I know of him. And although I'm not certain I've heard that he was spreading the word around about your relationship."

Davis jumped up from the sofa and paced the floor several times.

"Are you sure?" he asked worriedly.

"No. But then if I know, there might be others."

"I can't afford to let anything like that get around, Mr Blake. Not in my position. I know he's jealous as hell, and he might not stop at anything."

"You haven't been true to him, then?" I thoughtfully pursed my lips.

"Of course not! Why should I be?" He spoke bitterly.

"Maybe he's true to you and he expects the same kind of treatment."

"He's nothing but a spoiled brat!" It was odd to hear Davis speak that way. His voice was a rolling bass, and somehow, a voice like that is never associated with a homosexual. I didn't laugh, however. I was as grave about the situation as a young priest hearing his first confession.

"Do you think he wants to marry you?" I asked seriously.

"My God! I wonder if something like that is in the back of his mind! It's never come up, but such things are done, as you know . . . "

"He's only eighteen, actually, so that might be it." I said.

"And you should have it out with him, at any rate." I finished my drink and made another. I enjoyed the conversation and I'd given the old boy something to think about. It was asinine to me, but it was very serious to Jefferson Davis.

"I thought I knew Freddy," Davis said softly, "but maybe I don't know him at all. I've given him money, clothes, and only last week I gave him an early Picasso drawing for his . . . our anniversary. He was the one, now that I think of it, who remembered the anniversary of our, ah, relationship, and he surprised me with a gift of my favorite English preserves. Gooseberry, imported from England, you know. In my surprise, I retaliated with the drawing. He appeared pleased, and I know he was, although we had a terrible scene before the evening was over—"

"What was it about?"

Davis blushed; his crimson face was as bright as the pictures on the walls. "It was nothing of interest to you, I assure you. Just a foolish argument."

I got up from the sofa, finished my second drink on my feet, and placed the empty glass on the low table.

"To sum up, Mr Davis, you have a problem. You've got a jealous lover and you want to get rid of him. He's cramping your style, or rather, he's limiting your time. You'd like to get rid of him and you don't know how. Am I right or wrong?"

"You're right, that is, in a way, but I'm not so sure I want to get rid of Freddy. I'm rather fond of him, you know."

"Then I'll be running along. Thanks for the drinks, and I'd like to look at your paintings again some time. I don't know much about modern art and maybe you could explain some of it to me."

"I'd be glad to. Come in again, later tonight if you like." He squeezed my arm affectionately.

"Do you make a pitch for every man you meet?" I laughed. "I can see right now why Freddy's so jealous."

"I'm just trying to be friendly, Mr Blake," he said sternly. I had hurt his feelings.

"Thanks again for the drinks," I said. I opened the door and left the room. I felt greatly relieved to be free of him. Davis closed the door quickly and bolted it with the chain lock.

I walked down the carpeted hallway to the elevator and pushed the button. I waited patiently, watching the moving loops of cable through the glass of the door. Suddenly, from behind, a heavy blow struck me between the shoulder blades, and the force of the blow threw me against the door of the elevator. The wind was knocked out of me and I was partially paralyzed. I saw that I had been hit with a large fire extinguisher, and the nozzle of its rubber hose was spewing forth a frothy mixture over me as I lay on the floor. It was a brew of water, sulphuric acid and soda and it was ruining my blue gabardine suit. But until I could catch my breath I couldn't do anything about it.

A blond, chubby-faced young man, wearing gray slacks and a yellow sweater, was standing against the wall across the hallway. There was a sullen, righteous, frightened look on his fat face. His arms were spread, and the palms of his fleshy hands pushed hard against the wall behind him.

CHAPTER
7

My wind came back to me all at once and I took a deep grateful breath. With an effort I got to my feet and a sharp fiery pain seared my back. The handsome, chubby young man against the wall didn't attempt to run, but he didn't try to attack me again either. I approached him slowly, reached out quickly, and grabbed a handful of his yellow sweater with my left hand.

"You're Freddy Allen, aren't you?" I asked him, twisting the sweater a little more to get a better grip.

He nodded his head, once, and then, without warning, tears overflowed his pale blue eyes and rolled down his baby-fat, dimpled cheeks.

"You've taken him away from me!" He blubbered through his tears. "He doesn't love me anymore and it's your fault!"

Now, I don't really object to homosexuals. It's a big world and there is room for everybody. The way some men prefer to make love is their business, not mine, but it seemed to me that I was being used as a short blunt apex for a crazy triangle. I didn't like it and I didn't like Freddy. Davis was one type of homosexual and Freddy was another . . . Davis, at least, earned his own living, and he spread a certain amount of beauty in the world by selling art, explaining it, and enjoying it himself. But Freddy was nothing. He was a filthy leech. He had attached himself to Davis so firmly that the older man was desperate to break away. As I held Freddy against the wall and watched the juicy tears boil out of his eyes through his girlishly long lashes I was filled with loathing and aversion. And in addition to being an overly pretty, petty-minded kept boy, he had ruined my suit with a fire extinguisher . . .

I smashed my right fist into his face. His nose crushed noisily and blood spattered and smeared against his skin. His nose would never be termed aristocratic again. I hit him again in the face several times. After each blow he tried to scream, but before he could get it out I would hit him again. I didn't try to knock him out. I wanted him conscious; I wanted him to feel it. He covered his face, or tried to, with his left hand. I hit him again and the bones of his hand splintered. He dropped his hurt hand, screamed shrilly, and I loosened my grip on his sweater. He slumped weakly to the floor, cuddled his broken hand against his chest, and whimpered like a kicked dog, interspersing short, sharp yelps of pain between the whimpers. Without letting up any on his weird noises he put his right hand in his pocket, pulled out a knife with a spring button, pressed it, and the blade flipped out. He was fast with his leap to his feet. His legs had been gathered beneath him and he came up off the floor like a cat. The point of the long blade narrowly missed my throat. This was the excuse I needed to really clobber him.

Freddy whirled quickly after the missed thrust, crouched, and held his knife low at his side, looking for an opening. Patiently, flat-footed, I waited for him to make up his mind. He jumped forward, bringing the knife up awkwardly. I sidestepped his rush and chopped down on his wrist with the side of my right hand. The knife dropped to the rug and his rush carried him across the hallway. Following him up, I jerked his broken hand away from his chest and crushed it between both of mine. His whimpering ceased, the blood drained out of his face, and he turned white as a clown's makeup. He pitched forward to the floor. Unconscious.

I left Freddy lying in the hallway and ran up the stairs to the seventh floor instead of taking the elevator. I unlocked my door, entered, and undressed as quickly as I could. I didn't want to get burned by the sulphuric acid seeping through my suit. I showered again, using plenty of soap and hot water. As I toweled myself I examined my body carefully for red spots or burns. There weren't any, but there was a new blue bruise on my back where Freddy had hit me with the fire extinguisher.

If he had planned his attack with care I could have been seriously injured. In my life I'd been hit and nearly hit with a variety of weapons, but this was the first time anybody had ever used a fire extinguisher on me.

My blue gabardine was ruined. I felt more than a little unhappy about it. It was the first suit I'd bought when I got out of the army, and every time I wore it I was reminded of my freedom. I could never wear it again. I put on a white shirt, blue knitted tie, and my gray flannel suit. I wrapped the damp blue gabardine, pink shirt and cream necktie in a sheet of newspaper, put the bundle under my arm and left my room. I rode the elevator down to the lobby and left the hotel.

Walking up Powell Street, looking for a trash can, I was stopped by the red light at the corner. A maroon Ford was waiting for the light to change and I wedged the bundle between the rear bumper and the body of the car. The Ford moved out with the light change and took my suit with it. At the hack stand I dropped wearily into the rear seat of a cab and told the driver to take me to the Seal House.

The Seal House is at the beach and it overlooks a pile of rocks in the ocean. Seals spend a lot of time on that particular pile of rocks. And people interested in seeing seals over rocks flock to the Seal House restaurant to eat, drink, and look at the seals. I got a table by the window, ordered a drink and looked at the seals. It was almost six and the sun had gone down behind San Francisco. It still reflected its light on the ocean and turned the water into a flaky, shifty mirror. The seals, sprawled carelessly on the rocks, moved listlessly from time to time. Music by Muzak played softly over the speakers set in the four corners of the large dining room. My gin concoction arrived and I ordered another before the waitress got away from the table.

I was draining the dregs of my second drink when Florence

51

sat down across the table from me. She was breathing hard and it added freshness to her beauty. She was wearing a plain cobalt suit with two huge gunmetal buttons. She smiled, expelled a long breath, smiled again.

"I was looking for you in the bar," she said.

"When I come to the Seal House I watch the seals."

"Am I late?"

"I don't know. I haven't got a watch."

"Did you order dinner?"

"No. How do I know what you want to eat?"

"I always get the mixed seafood platter. Out of a mixture there's bound to be something good."

I ordered two mixed seafood plates, and two more drinks.

"Your father sent your bodyguards to see me today," I told her, to make conversation. "One of them said your old man wanted to talk to me."

Florence wore a puzzled expression. "He lied then. Father is in L.A. tonight. He flew down this afternoon to address a builders' association of some kind."

"Did you see him leave on the plane?"

"No, but I saw him leave the house. He left right before I called you at 2:30."

"It isn't the same. He might still be around. Of course, they might have lied as an excuse to take me somewhere and work me over again."

"Did they hurt you very much last night?" Florence asked solicitously.

"Not much. By the way, how did you get away? Or did you?" I looked over my shoulder with a mock terrified expression. Florence laughed, showing tiny sharp teeth.

"They're fired. After I told Daddy about you and I getting away last night he called them in and fired them."

"That may have been a blind . . . "

"No." She shook her head emphatically. "What good would it do?"

"I don't know." I grinned. "But if you aren't being followed anymore, I'm out of a job." I finished my drink.

"You've still got your job, Jake, if you insist on calling it that."

We both laughed. The seafood arrived and we let the conversation drop to pick around on the platters. The crab legs were good, but the sauce smelled like spoiled mayonnaise and olive oil. It tasted like spoiled mayonnaise and olive oil. I ordered coffee and lit a Camel.

"Want a dessert, Florence?"

"No." She lit one of my Camels with her Zippo lighter.

"I want to take you home with me. We can have dessert there."

"Suits me." We left the Seal House, walked to the parking lot, and climbed into her Buick.

"Where did you find your car?" I asked her.

"It was in the garage. I looked for it right after I called you this afternoon."

She drove across town, driving expertly, squeezing the big car in and out of places I didn't think it would fit in. I admire a good driver. I'm not a good driver myself and I've never owned a car. My sole driving experience has been limited to driving cars belonging to others, and not too much of that. When we reached her house she drove through the wrought iron gate and stopped in front of the entrance, putting the brakes on so hard the car skidded for three feet in the gravel of the driveway.

"It's the power brakes I had put in the other day," Florence said self-consciously. "I'm not quite used to them yet."

We entered the house. The living room was high-ceilinged, and an enormous, cut-glass chandelier lighted the farthest corner of the room like daylight. The room was of no particular period or design. Provincial chairs were mixed with mid-Victorian, and there was a low cocktail table carved out of a granite block and fitted with a polished marble top. It was about eight feet square and its legs were carved into griffin's feet. A set of Noh masks were on one wall, placed in imperfect alignment, and on another there was a scattering of swords, dirks and cutlasses. A Degas hung above the fieldstone mantel, depicting ballet girls in blue chalk, and the far, remaining wall was completely covered with a tapestry showing a crimson Roman army marching across a golden land.

It was an interesting room and I liked it. Florence mixed Martinis from a tray of bottles on the enormous stone table. I sat down on a seven-seat sofa that curved halfway around the table.

"I like your house, Florence."

"I hate it. It's too gloomy. Now, try this: I call it a Desert Wind. Nine-tenths gin, one-tenth vermouth. No olive. No onion. Nothing. just a toothpick."

I sipped the Desert Wind. "It's fair," I said, smiling, "only next time, skip the toothpick. The wood absorbs too much of the gin."

She sat down beside me and I put my arm around her. I finished my drink, took her glass, and set both of the glasses on the table. I picked her up and put her on my lap. She put her arms around my neck and I kissed her. We held the kiss until it got sloppy. I pushed her away from me.

"I'll have another Desert Wind," I said. My voice was dry.

"Me too." Her voice was high and small.

She poured the cocktails and as I reached for mine, a man came through the doorway from the hall. He was in his fifties, with powdery white hair, and an enormous, beakish nose. His skin was tight over high cheekbones, but it gathered and fell in folds on his chin and beneath his neck. His eyebrows were black and very heavy, and beneath his eyes there were huge blue-black circles. His hands looked too delicate for his short, thick-set body, and they were trembling. He wore a black tie, white shirt, and a white linen suit. He resembled a giant panda bear in reversed shades of white and black.

"So you're the private detective, Jake Blake—" His voice was shaking with an anger that was barely under control.

"Yes, sir," I said carefully, and I got up from the couch. "You must be Mr Weintraub . . . " I stuck my hand out to shake hands, but he ignored it completely and turned to snarl at Florence.

"Go to your room!" He told her fiercely.

"Fuck yourself," she remarked quietly and wandered over to the fireplace.

"I wanted to take a look at you, Blake," he said, ignoring Florence's suggestion. "I made arrangements to see you this afternoon, but you squirmed out of it some way—"

"I was in my office," I said. "If you wanted to see me, why didn't you call for an appointment instead of sending two thugs after me?"

"You're an unscrupulous man, Blake. I've checked on you, and I know how to handle your kind."

"Money won't do everything, Weintraub. Your daughter's twenty-six years old. If you think you can keep her under lock and key forever, you're—" I broke off in mid-sentence. Florence was laughing with whooping peals of choking laughter, and clutching the mantel for support. Weintraub looked blankly at me for a moment, and then held up his hand. It had stopped trembling.

"Daughter?" he asked vaguely. "Did she say she was my daughter?"

Florence stopped her laughter abruptly and stared at us sullenly.

"Well," I said. "Isn't she?"

"No. It so happens that Florence is my wife!" He glared suspiciously at me, still undecided as to whether I knew or didn't know she was his better half.

"Oh," I said. There was one more Desert Wind remaining in the glass pitcher. I poured it into my glass and drank it down.

CHAPTER
8

I remained as cool as I could, under the circumstances. Weintraub was watching me closely, looking for a reaction on my part that would prove me to be a liar. I set my empty glass on the table.

"Look, Mr Weintraub," I said feebly, "I didn't know she was your wife—"

Weintraub grimly set his lips and looked at Florence. She was standing in front of the fireplace; her arms were crossed beneath her considerable breasts, and her face bore a detached expression, as though she was thinking of something else.

"I believe you, Blake," Weintraub said with a trace of sadness in his voice. "A lot of her lovers didn't know she was married at first. But by the time they found out, she had them so completely—well, it's too late then. They don't want to give her up and I have to convince them that they'd better! It's all so—"

"Lies, lies. Lies, lies. Lies, lies. Lies, lies," Florence sing-songed.

"No, Blake, you're not the first of Florence's lovers by any means. And I really don't give a damn anymore what she does. If she had any discrimination, it wouldn't be so hard to take. But my wife doesn't draw the line," Weintraub said bitterly. "As far as she's concerned, there is no line! I've been forced to have her watched all the time. But that hasn't been, what you might call, practical . . . "

"If I'm so bad," Florence commented, "why don't you give me a divorce?"

Weintraub shook his massive head. "No, I'll never divorce you—and you don't want a divorce, anyway! You and I made an agreement, and that agreement was marriage. I got what I wanted and you got what you wanted. Money for you, and for me," he smiled sardonically, "the best sex in San Francisco!" He turned to me. "And as far as I'm concerned, it's worth every cent it's cost me!"

Weintraub's face was an angry red; his cheeks puffed, and his eyes brightened as though a switch was clicked on inside his head.

"I intend to protect my investment, Blake." He faced Florence. "Marriage is no different from any other type of contract. I'll fight to the last moment of my life for anything and everything I own. And if you tried to get a divorce, I have enough evidence on you to have you laughed out of court. Any court. You wouldn't get a penny, not even in a California court!"

He crossed the room briskly and jabbed a finger into my chest.

"Do you want to marry her, Blake? Do you think you could support her?"

"I don't know," I said honestly. "I've never given it any thought."

He sneered. His face was quite red in the places it wasn't blue-black. "You couldn't pay her doctor bills! Her sani—"

Florence screamed and cut him off. It was a startling, awesome outcry. Starting low in her chest, like a police siren heard in the distance, it gathered force and momentum and reached a terrifying crescendo. It stopped momentarily while she took another breath and then it started all over again. She exerted every muscle in her body to produce such a scream. Her eyes were closed and she stood with her feet apart and her fists clenched tightly; her elbows tight against her sides. It hurt my ears to listen to it. Taking Florence by the shoulders, I shook her back and forth as hard as I could. The hard shaking didn't even slow her down. I slapped her face three or four times.

"Stop it, Florence!" I had to yell at her to be heard.

I was knocked sideways across the room, hit from behind by Weintraub. I stumbled onto the stone table, banged my shin, and with luck, managed to remain on my feet. Weintraub had hit me just above my right kidney with a metal smoking stand. He swung the heavy stand again, but I evaded his clumsy swing by jumping backwards. The momentum of his charging swing whirled him around and I leaped forward with a looping right hand blow that caught him below the ear. He dropped the smoking stand and pitched forward to the floor. He didn't move.

"What's the matter with you, you crazy bastard!" I yelled. Florence had stopped screaming on Weintraub's fall, and my voice reverberated in the silent room. There was a sweet smile on Florence's face, and she wet her lips with the tip of her pink tongue.

"Do you think he's dead?" she asked excitedly.

"Of course not. What got into you, anyway?"

"I always scream when he starts to nag. It infuriates him and he usually goes away and leaves me alone." She rubbed her face ruefully. There was a large, red hand-mark on her face where I had slapped her. "You hurt me when you slapped me, but I don't mind."

"I thought you were hysterical, kid. Otherwise I wouldn't have done it."

"What difference does it make?" Florence shrugged comically. "As long as it's exciting." She sat down on the sofa, took a Marlboro out of the box on the table, and lit it with a table-lighter shaped like a miniature piece of Henry Moore's sculpture. "What about him, Jake?" she asked quietly, kicking her unconscious husband in the ribs with the point of her toe. "Is it worth the effort to bring him around?"

"I'll get some water. Where's the kitchen?"

"Through there." She pointed to the hallway and settled herself comfortably on the couch, puffing languidly on her cigarette.

I left the living room and wandered down the hall, holding

my hand tightly against my sore side to ease the pain. Weintraub had hit me with only a glancing blow of the smoking stand. A square, solid blow and I'd have been the one unconscious on the floor instead of him. Marriage or no marriage, he was nuts to hang onto a woman like Florence. But that was his business, not mine. Under the circumstances, I was through. No more playing around with Florence for me. A man like Weintraub had a lot of influence in San Francisco, and if he wanted to push things, I'd be relieved of my private investigator's license in a hurry. I'd bring him out of it, try my best to explain things quietly, and then I'd push off. This was the second time in one day that I had been sucked into a triangle through no fault of my own. And I didn't like it. The fifth door I tried led into the kitchen.

I got an empty saucepan out of the cabinet beneath the sink and filled it with cold water from the tap. I plucked a dish towel from the rack above the range and draped it over my arm. A cat meowed. There was a large charcoal-colored cat, with white feet, sitting on its haunches by the outside door. It meowed plaintively.

"Do you want out, Kitty?" I asked the cat. It meowed again. I put the pan of water down on the sideboard, crossed the kitchen and opened the door to the backyard. The stupid cat sat where it was without moving. I shut the door and picked up the pan of water again. The cat meowed again. I set the pan down again, opened the door so it could get out, but the cat didn't make a move. I kicked out with my right foot and caught the cat just right. It sailed out of the door, missed the steps completely and landed running. It quickly disappeared into the darkness of the backyard. I slammed the door and left the kitchen with the pan of cold water. I don't like cats, anyway. Too independent. And even when you try to do them a favor they don't appreciate it.

Florence was idly leafing through a movie magazine when I returned to the living room. She tossed the magazine on the table and looked curiously at the pan of water when I set it down.

"What are you going to do, Jake?"

Weintraub was still inert upon the floor. He was stretched

out, face down, with his arms spread. I turned him over on his back. It wasn't easy. He was heavier than he looked.

"I'm going to bring him to."

"Oh." Florence picked up her magazine again.

I wet the dishcloth and rubbed Weintraub's face with it. I slopped the cloth in water and wrung it out over his face. I slapped him lightly a couple of times. I dumped the entire panful of water over his face. There was a great deal of water in the pan and it made a pool beneath his head. He didn't stir a muscle. I searched among the many folds of skin on his neck for quite a while before I found his jugular vein. I couldn't feel a heartbeat, so I wasn't sure whether I had the vein or not. Lifting his right eyelid with my left hand I jabbed my right forefinger into his eye. No reflex. Florence's purse was at the other end of the table where I couldn't reach it.

"Hand me your little mirror," I told her, pointing to her handbag.

"Why?"

"I said to give me your mirror!" I was a little excited by that time and I had raised my voice. Florence opened her purse and handed me her compact. For a moment I couldn't open it, and when I found the latch, I was holding the compact upside down and rose-colored face powder was scattered over Weintraub's set expression. I held the mirror part of the compact as close as I could to Weintraub's lips, and then I examined it. There was no moisture or fogginess on the mirror. Not a trace. I snapped the compact shut and tossed it into Florence's lap.

"Is something wrong, Jake?"

"Yeah," I said, getting off my knees. I poured a double shot of gin into an empty glass and poured it down my throat. I choked slightly and the raw gin brought tears to my eyes. I wiped them away. Florence had lost interest in the movie magazine and was sitting on the edge of the sofa with her eyes widened. Her mouth was partly open, her lips wet.

"Is he dead, Jake?

"He couldn't be any deader."

CHAPTER
9

"Do you want a drink, Florence?"

"A little one." She indicated the size by holding up a thumb and forefinger an inch apart.

I poured a jigger of gin into a glass and handed it to her. I sat down across from her in a soft leather chair. But I leaped up immediately. Now was no time to sit down and relax. I had to figure an angle, and the best way for me to think is on my feet. I paced up and down the room, turning the facts over in my mind and getting nowhere.

"What do we do now, Jake?" Florence asked, after she gulped her drink and put the glass on the table. I didn't know.

"I don't know. I don't know what to do."

I took a cigarette out of the box on the table and lit it with the table-lighter. My hands trembled, and the cigarette tasted as dry as fifty-year-old sherry. After two drags I crushed the cigarette out in an ashtray.

"I suppose the smart thing to do is call the police, kid. But when I do my name is Fall Guy. There's a lieutenant who's been after me for a long time, and if I don't end up in the gas chamber, I'll end up at Folsom crushing stones. Somehow, the prospect of prison doesn't encourage me to do my right and proper duty as a citizen . . . "

"You and I both know it was an accident, Jake. But if I told the truth, nobody would believe me. Milton and I have had some nasty arguments in our time, and his lawyer has some papers in his office that would—well, all I can say, is that this is very unfortunate."

"That's a good word for it. Unfortunate."

"I know what we can do, Jake. We can leave."

"Leave? Where would we go?"

"There are lots of places."

"Not anymore, there aren't. Twenty years ago a person could disappear, but not now. We might get away for awhile, but we'd be caught, and then it would be just that much tougher."

"What about me? I don't want to die . . . " Florence started to cry. I sat down beside her and tried to give her some comfort by putting my arms around her.

"Come on, Florence, crying isn't going to do you any good. The best thing to do is call the police. When they get here, we clam up, say absolutely nothing. Let them jump to a lot of wrong conclusions. Then, after we get a lawyer, we tell the exact truth and hope for the best—"

"No!" Florence pulled away from me and got to her feet. She glared down at me, and stood with her legs apart, arms akimbo. "Do you think I'm going to rot in prison over a son-of-a-bitch like him?" She kicked Weintraub's body viciously with her toe. "Take a good look at him! Go ahead! How'd you like to have something like that crawl into bed with you every night?" She turned away from me. "He was always sweating. Not a hot, decent sweat, the way a working man sweats—oh, no, not him! It was a cold, clammy sweat, and his skin is just like a frog's. I put up with it, just the way he said I did; for the money, and I've got that money too. He thought he was so smart!" she said derisively. "He never gave me any cash, you see, but he gave me charge accounts in every store and restaurant in town. So I figured out a system . . . "

She paused for breath, laughed wildly.

"It's a simple system, really. I'd buy a dress, or furs, something expensive—say a hundred dollars or so, and then I'd sell it back to the salesgirl for half price without taking it out of the store. The girl could sell it and make twice the profit for herself. See? I'd charge the hundred dollars and get fifty in cash from the salesgirl. Milton never complained about bills, and there was so much stuff I sent home anyway, besides the stuff I sold for cash, he never got wise to what I was doing. At least I don't think he did."

"How much money have you got?"

"Plenty."

"How much?"

"I don't know exactly."

"How much?"

"Five thousand dollars in the vault at the Desert Sands in Vegas. Another ten thousand in Mexico City, and five thousand in a safe deposit box in New York."

"That much?"

"That much, and maybe more."

It was enough money for me to think things over a little more carefully. In fact, twenty thousand dollars was a fabulous sum to a man like me. The most money I'd ever had in a lump sum was eight hundred dollars. That was my discharge pay when I got out of the army, and I hadn't hung onto it long enough to really get a good look at it. Maybe Florence and I could work things out, at that. If we picked up the five thousand in Vegas, it would be easy to get to Mexico City. Once in Mexico, we could live for a long time on fifteen thousand dollars. At least long enough for the hunt to die down. Then we could quietly move to New York and lose ourselves in the masses. To stand trial and avoid conviction was a thirty-to-one shot. A jury might take a dim view of a so-called accident if it found out I was sleeping with the wife. And as far as claiming self-defense, a jury might figure Weintraub was entirely within his rights to bounce a smoking stand off my ribs. After all, a husband is justified in slugging a man who is fondling his wife when he isn't supposed to be at home. One lousy, indignant husband, or one church-going wife on the jury could put me behind the bars on a second degree rap, if nothing else. Ten years. Ten years in jail would raise my age to forty-three instead of thirty-three. And I had already wasted ten years of my life in the army. Florence was right. It was best to leave quietly and hope for the best while we were out of jail instead of in . . .

"Please, Jake," Florence said, putting her arms around my waist and burying her face against my chest. "I'll make it up to you. You'll see."

"I know you will, Florence. And I'll make it up to you for putting the last punch in your meal ticket."

Florence blew her nose on a piece of Kleenex she took out of her purse. She took a tiny brush and her lipstick and made a new, coral mouth. I poured another shot of gin in my glass, but I didn't drink it. If we were going to be on the run for awhile, I thought it best to dispense with drinking.

"How long do you think we have, Florence?"

"What do you mean?"

"I mean servants! I know damned well you don't do the housework in this place."

"We should have until Monday morning, at least. There's a housekeeper, Mrs Watkins, and a maid, but I let them go for the weekend as soon as Milton left for the airport. The damned liar! I wanted us to have the place to ourselves."

I walked across the room to the large picture window, pulled the drapes aside slightly and looked outside. The circular driveway was empty except for Florence's Buick. There was a streetlight near the entrance to the grounds, but I didn't see anyone lurking about on the street or near the gate.

"What about those two clowns? Do you think he actually fired them? It's hard to tell."

"I think he did, Jake. As he said, what good were they?"

"I wish I knew for sure. They told me he wanted to talk to me when they tried to pick me up at the hotel. And he sort of admitted that he sent them for me. Of course, he could have fired them afterward."

"No. They were fired when I told you, all right. He must have asked them later to go on that one more errand."

"But they know all about us, baby. And if they tell the police the situation, we'd never prove to a jury that I hit Weintraub in self-defense."

"You don't have to convince me, Jake. I know I'm in this as deep as you are. I'm ready to go."

"I am too. I was thinking out loud. And I certainly don't want to be tailed on our way to Vegas."

"Let's skip Vegas and drive straight through to Mexico City."

"What about the dough in Vegas? I don't have enough money to get to Mexico. If we pick up the money in Vegas, we can charter a plane to drop us below the border."

"Whatever you say, Jake. You're the man, and it's up to you to decide."

"Then let's get going. Pack a bag with a few things, and the sooner we leave the better."

Florence kissed me quickly on the mouth and ran up the stairs. To make certain, I checked Weintraub again. He was dead all right. No mistake. He hadn't hit his head, so it must have been my right to the head that killed him. His face looked strange with the rose face powder sprinkled over it. It was like seeing again the first dead man I'd seen in Europe. He had been in the same position as Weintraub, only lying beside the road. The dust from the moving column had powdered his face almost the same shade of rose. Eyeballs and all. I shoved Weintraub's body under the table so that the head was out of sight. I didn't want to look at it.

It would be unwise to stop at a restaurant on the drive to Vegas, so I returned to the kitchen for a look inside the refrigerator. There was part of a ham, six tomatoes and an almost full jar of mayonnaise. I found a loaf of bread in the bread box and a table knife in a drawer beside the sink. I put this stuff in a paper sack and returned to the living room. We could make sandwiches on the road.

Florence came down the stairs with a small over-nighter in her hand. She was wearing a full-length mink coat over her suit. I took the small suitcase and she got her purse from the table. After

I switched out the lights, we left the house and got into the Buick. I threw the over-nighter on the back seat and Florence drove through the gates. I kept my eyes open, but there was nobody on the street, and there were no cars parked near the house.

"Never mind stopping at my hotel, Florence. Head straight for the 101 bypass."

"I knew something like this would happen someday," Florence giggled. "Wasn't I smart to put some money away, here and there, just in case?"

"Yeah," I said. "Roll up your window. It's cold, and I'm not wearing a mink coat."

CHAPTER
10

I have to give Florence some credit, but not much. She didn't start speeding until we cleared the traffic of the city and reached the wide four lanes of the 101 bypass. When we hit the bypass she floor-boarded the accelerator and passed everything in front of her. I found myself pressing the floorboard with my right foot as though I had a brake of my own. I was forced to say something to her.

"Listen, Florence. If we get picked up for speeding we'll be taken to the nearest jail. And once we're in jail we won't get very far on our trip to Mexico City."

"Nobody can catch us!" she exclaimed. "Nobody. Just let them try!"

"I don't want them to try. Now, slow down!"

Reluctantly she slowed to sixty miles an hour, and we coasted through the thirty-five mile zone of San Jose at this reduced speed. On the other side of this little city we were back to two-lane traffic and she was forced to keep the car at a reasonable speed. I was more relaxed and I'd stopped looking nervously out the rear window. I hadn't seen anybody following us anyway, and even if they had, they would have been lost long before we reached San Jose. I made two huge sandwiches from the ham, tomatoes, mayonnaise and bread. They hit the spot and we wolfed them down hungrily, Florence driving with one hand.

"You were brilliant, Jake," Florence admitted, "to think of food. I never would have thought of it."

"A man should use his head. That's what it's for." I lit a

cigarette from the dashboard lighter and settled back against the soft leather seat.

"Light me one," Florence said. I started to light another Camel from mine and she shook her head. "No, one of mine. They're in my purse." I opened her purse and found her Marlboros and lighted one of them. I was forced to dig for the cigarettes because she had so much junk in her purse: Kleenex, Midol tablets, book matches, compact, lipstick, keys, a chamois cloth full of jewelry, and a tiny, pearl-handled .25 caliber pistol. It was a semi-automatic, loaded with a magazine containing seven rounds.

"What's with the pistol?" I asked her.

"I thought it might come in handy so I brought it along."

"Do you know how to use it?"

"I've fired it a few times. Put it back."

I dropped the pistol back into her purse and zipped the zipper. I noticed a clock on the wall of a filling station as we whipped by. It was 10:30. The time had really passed in a hurry. It was hard to believe it was that late, and at the same time, so much had happened, it was hard to believe it was that early. We were well down 101, the other side of Salinas, and the big trucks crowded the highway. We pulled up behind a wide semi- and followed it for five full minutes at twenty miles an hour. The string of back lights on its right side blinked on and off several times and Florence stuck her head out the window.

"Don't worry! We won't!" she screamed at the top of her voice at the truck up ahead of us.

"What're you yelling about?" I asked.

"I was telling the driver we wouldn't try to pass him!" She was quite excited. "His signals," she explained. "When he blinks his lights like that he's telling us a car is coming and not to pass. See?" A car passed us going north. "That car was coming and he was telling us about it with his lights."

"But why did you scream at him? He can't hear you."

"He might be able to . . . "

"Never," I said.

She had calmed down. "I know all of the truck signals, every one. I used to know a truck driver and he explained them to me. They have signals for turns, slow down, speed up, police ahead, weighing ahead, all kinds of things."

"What kind of signal do they use when they want to pull off and take a leak?"

"What's that?" She looked at me sharply.

"Never mind. He's blinking again."

She blinked her lights back, we passed the truck, and as we passed the cab she blinked the headlights twice more. The truck driver blinked his headlights twice in return.

"I blinked 'thank you,'" she said proudly, "and he blinked 'that's all right.'"

"That's just fine," I said.

"It's common courtesy. If people used road courtesy the way truck drivers do, there wouldn't be any accidents. They are the noblemen of the highway."

"You must have been mighty impressed by the truck driver you knew," I said, bored by the subject.

"He was a gentleman in every respect," she said solemnly.

I hadn't realized it before, but Florence Weintraub was just about as dumb as a woman could get. When it came to any thinking, I realized, I would have to do it all. At this time I thought about the license tags. As soon as the alarm went out, the tag numbers and description of the car would be teletyped to every city and county sheriff in the U.S. There were a lot of Buick Roadmasters, but only one license number to look for.

"Some time after midnight, Florence, we'd better exchange these license plates."

"How?"

"Trade them with another car. By the time they find out about the switch it'll be too late to do anything about it."

"If you trade with another car, the owner will know right away, won't he?"

"No." I grinned. "I'll trade with a parked car, a car on a

used car lot. That way it won't be noticed until after the car is sold. See?"

"I never would have thought of that!" Florence said admiringly.

"Naturally," I said, reaching over and patting her on the leg. "We're going to beat this thing yet, kid. Just stick with me."

"I am sticking with you. I think you're wonderful and let's stop the car right now and take a little nap."

"It might be a good idea at that. We can spare an hour."

Florence dropped the speed down to thirty miles an hour. After about a mile I spotted a dirt road curving off the highway into a grove of young eucalyptus trees. The trees were not over ten or fifteen feet high, but they were planted close enough together to provide cover from the highway.

"Pull in there, baby," I ordered, pointing, and Florence turned onto the dirt road, twisted the wheels to the left sharply, and we ploughed into the grove of young trees like a tank. We crushed trees down for thirty yards and then she cut the engine. All of a sudden it was very silent and very dark. A moment later the disturbed crickets began to rub their legs together noisily and I rubbed Florence's legs beneath her skirt.

"What do you think?" I asked her.

"I think it's a wonderful idea," she answered, shrugging out of her mink coat.

I found a clear spot near the car and spread the plaid lap robe on the grass. We undressed, shivering in the cold night air. We stretched out on the blanket and I pulled the mink coat over us. The blanket on the bottom kept the dampness of the grass away and we were warm in an instant. It wasn't a bit like the time on the porch of the nightclub. We had plenty of time and we took it. We both knew what we were doing and we tried several things before we decided on one we both liked best.

Afterward, I was warm and comfortable, and lay there smoking a cigarette, and Florence snuggled next to me with her head on my chest.

"Give me a drag on your cigarette."

I handed Florence my cigarette. I felt sorry for her. She was in trouble. What had her husband tried to tell me about doctor bills? Something about sanitation—sanity?

"Let's go!" I leaped to my feet, taking the mink coat with me.

"You're mean!" Florence laughed. We dressed hurriedly. I held her coat for her, folded the blanket, and we got back into the car. She backed slowly through the trees to the dirt road, forward to the highway and turned right. The Buick had a quick pick-up and we were soon driving south at eighty miles an hour.

When we reached Santa Maria I told her to look for a used-car lot. There were a couple on the main drag, but there were still a few people on the street and I didn't want to take a chance removing a set of plates at either one of the well-lighted lots. She turned off the main street, which was also Highway 101, and we found a small used-car lot two blocks away. I found a pair of pliers in the trunk and slipped them into my pocket. Florence stayed in the car, parked at the curb, where she could act as lookout. I was on my knees, with the pliers in my hand, behind a 1934 Olds when Florence honked the horn. When I looked up quickly, a man in an O.D. watchman's uniform was standing less than three feet away from me. He was in his fifties, and his face was a kindly, weather-beaten brown. He wore a red necktie with his uniform instead of a regulation black or blue.

"What're you doing, son?" he asked. He wasn't wearing a gun, but he idly swung a billy back and forth.

"How are you tonight, officer?" I asked him.

"I'm fine. What're you doing, son?"

"I sold this car to Mr Darstadt," I said. The name of the car lot was Jack Darstadt's Quick Deal Used Cars, and the name was painted in red on a blue background, on a sign that ran the length of the lot. "He only paid me eighty-five bucks, Officer, and I thought I'd drop around tonight to see how much he marked it up. You see, I wanted to see what kind of a deal he made me."

Charles Willeford

The watchman walked to the front of the car and I got off my knees and put the pliers back in my pocket. He looked curiously at the price marked on the windshield in whitewash.

"He's selling it for $135. Looks like you were took. What were you doing with the pliers?"

"I don't like being took," I said ruefully. "I was planning on taking my spotlight back to sort of get even . . . "

The watchman shook his head and smiled. "I can't let you do that, son. I know just how you feel. These used-car salesmen'll take your eyeteeth if you let 'em. But tryin' to get back at 'em in the middle of the night ain't no way to do it. You got yourself a dirty deal maybe, and maybe you didn't. But it's best to forget about it. Now you go on and get in your car and move on along. There's a pretty girl waitin' on you, and you don't want to get her mixed up in no mess like this."

"Yes, sir. I was sore about the deal I got, that's all."

"Two wrongs don't make one right, son."

"Yes, sir. Well, thanks, Officer."

"Goodnight, son."

I climbed back into the Buick and shut the door. The watchman watched us from the car lot until we pulled away.

"We'll get the tags in Santa Barbara," I told Florence.

"What did he say to you?"

"He said to move along."

In Santa Barbara I exchanged the tags without any trouble at a car lot on lower State Street. Afterwards, we drove on, heading for Los Angeles. I was getting sleepy and I put my head back on the seat, trying to doze off. Florence jolted me awake.

"Jake, when we get to Vegas, let's get married."

"Why?" I said, sitting up straight.

"Because I love you, Jake, and that's the God's truth."

I lit cigarettes, a Marlboro for her and a Camel for me. I thought it over.

I really thought it over.

CHAPTER
11

The word I-D-E-A-L floated across the surface of my mind. I hadn't thought of that key word since I'd left the service. It was the key to the five-paragraph field order. If you followed it, nothing was left out; your thoughts were organized, and your orders to subordinates were clear, curt and complete. Maybe I could remember it . . .

I. *Information.* That was easy. Information of the enemy and friendly troops. My enemy was the law. All law and the personnel having anything to do with law enforcement. The enemy was Melvin and Ferguson, the two bodyguards who knew I was mixed up with Florence. The enemy was Milton Weintraub, even though he was dead. The enemy was the watchman in Santa Maria who might remember me and recognize me. There were other enemies back in San Francisco. Barbara Ann Allen and her fairy brother, Freddy. Police Lieutenant Pulaski. Who else? Myself. Sure. A man is always his own worst enemy. I'd have to be careful so I wouldn't give myself away. Enemy weapons? The Buick. This very comfortable big, blue car could give us away, even with its change of license tags. Florence. The money Florence had stashed away. I could count money and Florence among my friends. Until I could exchange Florence for the money, she was the only friend I had. Except one. Myself. In addition to being my worst enemy I was also my best friend.

D. *Decision.* This was the decision of the commander or the overall picture of the situation. I was the commander as well as the troops. The big picture or idea was to get as far away as possible before the body was discovered. And en route, get the money. My objective was Mexico City with fifteen thousand bucks in my pocket. And perhaps a change of name. Jake Blake was a hard, harsh-sounding name. So far, I'd lived up to it. It would be best to change it. Jake Blake is too easy to remember.

E. I couldn't remember what E stood for. It meant the orders to be issued to subordinates after getting the Information of enemy and friendly troops, and the Decision of the commander. But the exact meaning of E escaped me. Expedient? Expedite? Entourage? What difference did it make? I'd issue my orders to myself anyway. Right now, my orders to myself were to go along with the gag . . .

A. *Ammunition*. In the fourth paragraph of the field order you were supposed to tell where the ammunition dump was, the weapons to be used, what kind of artillery support you could expect, and other backing. Well, Florence had a .25 caliber pistol. Mine was in my hotel room. If I took Florence's pistol away from her she might get suspicious. Let her keep it. She was my only friend. I'd keep it that way. As far as the support I could expect, there wasn't any. My wits, and that was all. Ammunition was money. When I got the money I'd have all the ammunition I'd need . . .

L. *Liaison*. Where the command post is located. How the messages are supposed to be transmitted. The police had a wire and telephone service that would stretch anyplace they wanted it to reach. As long as we were in the U.S. we would be in danger. Even in the Vegas melting pot, where nobody checked on anybody, we would be in danger. But from there we could get a plane to Mexico. I didn't know how, but money talks, and money could charter us a plane. My contact was Florence. The smart thing to do was to keep the line tight. As tight as possible.

"Florence, baby," I said, keeping my voice fairly low so that it would sound husky with emotion and sincerity, "I fell in love with you the moment you walked through the door of my office. And everything I've done since has only increased my love for you. It makes me a little ashamed that you were the one to suggest marriage instead of me. I want you to be my wife more than anything else in the world. I love you, cherish you, and I'll try to make you happy for the rest of your life, no matter what happens." For an additional effect, I blew my nose.

Florence was crying softly. I passed her my handkerchief.

"Oh, Jake," she cried, wiping her eyes, "I don't know what I'd have done if you refused. I do love you so. I'll admit I married Milton for his money, and I haven't always been on the up and up with anybody else either. I never worked in a house and I never worked the street, but I was almost at that point when I met Milton. I was working as a B-girl in a bar on Howard Street. And . . . sometimes. . ." It was hard for Florence to make this confession. "I did it for money sometimes, but it was because I wanted to eat. That's the only reason."

"Sure, baby," I said, patting her on the shoulder. "I understand. What the hell, I've been around. What you did before doesn't make any difference to me. We're starting a new life together in another country, and all that's past is past."

"I wanted you to know." She wasn't crying anymore. Now that her conscience was relieved she was happy.

"Don't even think about it. From now on it's us two and that's all. As soon as we reach Vegas, before we do anything else, we'll get married. Now I'm going to take a little nap. When you get tired of driving, wake me, and I'll take over."

"Put your head on my shoulder and go to sleep, Jake. Driving never makes me tired. I love it."

I put my head on her shoulder, stretched my legs out as far as I could, and I was asleep before I knew it.

● ● ●

I awoke at dawn and looked out the window. We were in the desert. The landscape looked like a crumpled winding sheet dotted with dead flies. The flies were the dark, scattered growths of cacti that were barely visible in the first light of morning. My mouth tasted like sour wine and my temples painfully throbbed. My neck was stiff and my legs were cramped. Both feet were asleep. I stamped them up and down on the floorboards to relieve the stinging sensation.

"Where are we?" I asked Florence.

"About fifty miles from Vegas." She smiled. Her eyes were red rimmed and sore looking.

"Why didn't you wake me so you could take a nap yourself?"

"I can't sleep in a moving car, so I just let you sleep. Believe me, you did all right!"

"How far are we from Vegas?" I asked again.

"About fifty miles."

I whistled. "You must have driven like mad!"

"It's easy to make good time on the desert."

"What's on the radio?" I switched it on and while it warmed up I lit a cigarette. The radio hummed into life and an announcer recommended a brand of dog food, finished his pitch and let a platter go for some music. I pushed a button for another station.

"What are you doing with the radio on?" Florence exclaimed.

"I want to hear the news, see if they discovered the body—"

"Turn it off!"

"Why? There might be some news—"

"I said turn it off!" Florence screamed at me. She leaned forward and turned the radio off herself. It made me sore.

"What's the matter with you?" I reached for the knob.

Florence bent down, keeping her left hand on the wheel, and removed her right slipper with her free hand. She banged the heel of her slipper against the face of the radio until the glass broke. She dropped her slipper, jerked the two knobs off the radio (the knobs for tune and volume) and tossed them out of the window. Her face was angry.

"When I tell you I don't want the radio on, Jake, I mean it!"

"I guess you do at that. But why?"

"I don't need a reason."

"And you don't have any either." She was a screwball in a lot of ways, no doubt about it. I sulked for awhile, then thought better of it. No use antagonizing the woman.

"I'm sorry, kid," I said. "There probably isn't any news anyway."

"I'm the one who's sorry, Jake. I'm tired, that's all, and I didn't feel like listening to any yapping."

"Sure. I know how you feel. Forget it."

Once the sun comes up in the desert it rises fast. It hung on the horizon like a solid neon pumpkin, beaming through our windshield. It grew warmer all the time. The closer we got to Vegas, the more numerous the billboards. Every club, every gambling hall claimed to be better than the last one advertised. Each claimed to have better entertainment than the last. As I remember Vegas, it was a good town. I hadn't been there for several years, but I'd had a good time, even though I ended up by hitchhiking to Los Angeles to get away.

When we reached the outskirts, Florence slowed to forty miles an hour. I looked for a motel without a NO VACANCY sign.

"If we can find a vacancy we'd better grab it," I said. "We can get married afterwards."

"Do you think a motel is better than one of the hotels?"

"Certainly. You don't meet people in a lobby when there isn't any lobby. It's our best bet."

A car pulled out of a motel called the "Home Rest Motel" and headed east.

"Pull in there," I told Florence.

"There's a NO VACANCY sign—"

"I can see it. But that car's pulling out and we can get the cabin they vacated."

Florence turned sharply and skidded to a stop in the thick, white gravel that covered the patio of the motel. I got out of the car and pushed the night-bell by the side of the door at the cabin marked OFFICE. I waited. After awhile, a man so small he narrowly missed being a dwarf, opened the door and smiled up at me.

"I'm sorry, sir," he said pleasantly, "we don't have a vacancy." He turned away, scratching himself under his pajama top.

"A car just left. We'll take that cabin." I pointed to the empty garage at the end of the row next to Cabin Six.

"It isn't fixed up yet. Won't be ready till ten, anyway."

"We'll take it. We've got to get married first, so by the time we get back from the ceremony you can have it ready."

"That's different!" His wrinkled little face took on new interest. He opened the screen door for me and I signed the register *Mr John Smith and Wife*. He smiled and nodded his head up and down. He gave me four one dollar bills in exchange for a ten.

"Now, Mr Smith," he said, "have you made your arrangements for getting married?" He had a nice voice, very pleasant.

"No, but I understand it isn't much of a problem."

"Not if you know how to go about it. Suppose you and—?"

"Mary Brown."

"All right. Suppose you and Miss Brown come on into my little kitchen here and drink some coffee? I'll call up Luke's and take care of you, get things arranged."

"Who is Luke?"

"One of the best. He gives the nicest ceremony in Vegas."

"Friend of yours?"

"We throw a little business to each other now and then. His ceremony is very nice, though, and I know you and Miss Brown will like it. And as long as you're getting married anyway, might as well let Luke do it. He don't charge no more than anybody else, and his connections cut corners on the license. By the time you get there everything'll be set."

"Go ahead, Mr—"

"Anderson. Shorty Anderson."

"Call Luke, then." I returned to the car and Florence raised her eyebrows.

"We're all set, Florence. Shorty's calling Luke to arrange the wedding for us, and we've got the cabin."

"Who is Luke?"

"I don't know, but as long as he's authorized to give weddings, I don't see what difference it makes."

We entered the office cabin and hesitated inside the door. Shorty was talking on the telephone. He covered the mouthpiece with his hand. "Go right into the kitchen. I made that coffee on the stove fresh last night, so all you gotta do is light a match under it."

I heated the coffee and Florence and I had a cup apiece before the little man joined us in the kitchen. He smiled admiringly at Florence, solemnly shook hands with both of us.

"It's all arranged. And when you get back your cabin'll be ready. It isn't every day I get newlyweds, but when I do I'm just as pleased as punch. Planning to stay long?"

"Maybe a week," I said, pouring more coffee into my cup.

"Well, that's just fine." He gave us directions to Luke's and we left the motel.

On the drive through town to Luke's, Florence grew suspicious of the little man. "Do you think he suspects anything?"

"How could he? He's been asleep all night."

"It didn't help any for you to sign the register as John Smith."

"You're wrong. Nobody uses John Smith anymore because it's so common. The same with Mary Brown. You pick a fancy name to use and they know right away it's a phony."

"You're probably right. But John Smith, Mary Brown— *Jesus!*"

Luke was a middle-aged man with a pale complexion, a dark mustache and long, thin fingers. He was dressed for the ceremony in a dark blue silk suit with a red carnation in the buttonhole of the jacket. The papers were ready and we signed them, John Smith and Mary Brown, in the places he indicated. Luke led the way into the tiny chapel adjoining his living room and took his place behind a waist-high rostrum in front of a life-sized painting of Jesus Christ. The picture was amateurish, and the artist had painted the eyes so that they seemed to follow you no matter where you happened to be in the tiny chapel. Luke's wife, a heavy, buxom blonde, was seated at a Hammond electric organ, and as we entered the chapel she started to play *Rock of Ages.*

"Never mind the music," I told her. "Let's get on with it."

A man I hadn't noticed before was sleeping on the long bench that ran the width of the rear of the room. Luke apologized.

"I woke him up as soon as Shorty called, but he must have gone back to sleep again. I know he don't look so good, but lots of times I have to marry people in the middle of the night and a witness is a witness. You can give him a little gambling money after the ceremony if you want. That's the reason he sleeps here, just to get a little gambling money."

Luke woke the man by pulling his legs off the bench and standing him on his feet with one swift motion. He blinked his eyes and stumbled into his place at my right. Mrs Luke left the organ and stood at Florence's left. The witness reeked of gin and had a three-day stubble of beard on his face. I pushed him away from me.

"Don't stand so close," I told him.

Luke opened a small, white book and read the ceremony. It was very short, but as Shorty had said, it was nice. Luke read it rapidly in a deep, falsely emotional tone of voice, and parts of it were hard to follow.

He paused. "Do you have a ring?"

"I'm wearing it already," Florence said for me.

"Fine. I pronounce you man and wife." We shook hands all around and Mrs Luke kissed Florence on the cheek. I gave the gin-soaked witness a dollar bill and he left the chapel muttering under his breath.

The ceremony, including the license fee, cost me ten dollars, and I tipped Luke another five. Luke waved to us from the doorway as we climbed into the Buick. On the way back to the motel we stopped at a drive-in and ate breakfast at the inside counter. Florence complained about the wedding all during breakfast.

"It was the lousiest wedding I've ever seen," she grumbled.

"Don't let it bother you, Mrs Smith," I said, grinning.

"You're lucky to get rid of a name like Brown in exchange for a nice one like Smith." I left the counter and lost four quarters in the slot machine by the cash register while Florence finished her coffee.

We returned to the motel.

Shorty was coming out of our cabin as Florence pulled into the garage. I got her bag out of the backseat and Shorty took it out of my hand and led us into the cabin. He put the bag at the foot of the bed on the little stand, spread his arms wide. "There you are, folks. I told you it wouldn't take long. Now, if you need anything, just holler. Your bed's been changed and there's plenty of extra towels in the bathroom. Congratulations, Mr Smith, and you too, Miss." We shook hands and he backed out of the door and closed it.

"What is he, a dwarf or what?" Florence asked.

"I don't know and I care less. All I want is sleep." I undressed and climbed into the big, soft double bed. Florence went into the bathroom for a shower and I was asleep before she came out. She woke me by nibbling on my ear with her sharp teeth.

"Cut it out," I said sleepily. "I'm too tired."

"Is that any way to treat your wife on your wedding day, Mr Smith?" She was naked and not quite dry from her shower. She pressed her damp body as close to me as she could get it.

"Now, look. I told you I'm tired and I mean it. Let's forget about it for now and take a little nap. After we're rested there will be plenty of time. Then we can pick up the five thousand at the Desert Sands; and tonight I'll see about getting us a plane out of here."

"What five thousand?" The surprise in her voice was genuine.

I was very tired. There was fatigue in every bone and muscle of my body, and I was in a deep, soft bed. But when I heard that tone of surprise I was suddenly wide-awake. Any and all thoughts of sleep were gone. I sat up in bed.

"The five thousand dollars you've got in the safe at the Desert Sands." I said it slowly so there wouldn't be any misunderstanding.

"I don't have any money in Vegas. What are you talking about?"

"Easy now, baby. You told me definitely that you had five thousand at the Desert Sands Hotel, another ten in Mexico City, and five in a safe deposit box in New York. Now what about it?" I didn't raise my voice but there was a slight quaver in it.

"I didn't tell you that," she said indignantly.

"Yes, you did."

"No, I didn't either."

I didn't go on with it. I lit a cigarette and started dressing. All right. So she was crazy.

"Where are you going?" Florence asked worriedly.

"Out."

"Listen to me, Jake. I don't remember telling you anything like that. I've never even been here before, so why would I tell you a lie like that?"

"I don't know, but that's what you said."

"I *have* got ten thousand dollars in Mexico City!"

"You've never been to Mexico City."

"I was too! I was there all last summer with Milton. We stayed at the Casa del Oro Hotel. My money's in the safe there. If you don't believe me I'll send a wire and prove it to you!"

"Sure. And let the police know that the widow Weintraub is staying at the Home Rest Motel in Vegas under the name of Mrs John Smith."

"How else can I prove it to you?"

"I don't know. I don't think you can." I tied my necktie and slipped into my jacket.

"Where're you going? You're not going to leave me here?"

"No. I wouldn't do that. We're in this together, baby. But I'm going to get a drink and do a little thinking. Things are different now."

"I'll go with you." She threw the covers back and got out of bed.

"No. I don't want you with me. Get some sleep. You need it and I had some in the car. I want to do my thinking by myself."

I sat down in a chair and bent down and tied my shoes. When I looked up, Florence had her little pistol in her hand and she was pointing it in my face. Standing naked before me, she resembled a teenaged girl except for the black, coarse mat of hair between her legs that curled into a lopsided triangle halfway up her stomach. The ends of the long, white scars on her belly extended well down into the pubic hair. I raised my eyes to hers and stared at her for a full minute before I said anything.

"If you're going to shoot, go ahead."

The pistol wavered and she lowered her arm, dropped the pistol onto the carpet.

"You aren't going to leave me, are you, Jake?"

"I said I wasn't." I got up from the chair, put my arms around her and kissed her hard on the mouth. "Don't get excited, baby. I'll be back after awhile. I've got to think things out, that's all. Now get back into bed and go to sleep. Okay?"

"I wouldn't know what to do if you left me."

"I'm not going to leave you." I picked her up, dumped her on the bed and pulled the covers up to her chin. I kissed her again. "I'll be back in about an hour." She rolled over and put her face into the pillow. I left the cabin, closing the door soundlessly behind me.

As I walked through the white gravel to the highway the full impact of my stupidity sank in. How dumb could a man get and still go on living?

CHAPTER
12

By the time I had crunched down the line of cabins and reached the highway I was almost sick to my stomach. I stopped for a moment and looked up and down the highway. A drink was what I needed. The Dry Bones Cabaret was the first joint down The Strip; two hundred yards away. I made for it, wiping the perspiration from my forehead with my handkerchief.

I had been played for a sucker and I didn't like it. Florence had what she wanted, although why she wanted to marry me was more than I could figure out. Of course, we were in it together, both equally guilty under the law, but just the same . . . then it hit me, and I laughed. Now that we were married neither one of us could testify against the other. That must have been the reason. I felt a little better. After all a rule like that worked both ways. Maybe she *did* have ten thousand dollars stashed away in Mexico City.

Well, I'll never know now.

I entered the Dry Bones Cabaret. It was plush. It had a wine-colored wall-to-wall carpet underfoot, a gold leaf bas-relief chase of cowboys and Indians circling the wall, and every form of gambling going on that you could think of except horse racing. The gambling room was jammed. There were women in shorts, slacks and evening dress, and there were men in shorts, slacks and evening dress. A few conservatives like myself were wearing ordinary business suits. But everyone was gambling.

I headed straight for the bar and ordered a double Tom Collins. The air-conditioning helped some, but I was still hot from my short walk in the desert sun. I cooled off ten degrees merely by shaking the ice cubes in my tall drink. I downed it, ordered another. The tariff for the two drinks was cheap, much cheaper than I had thought it would be, and for a moment I was surprised. Then I remembered that the top entertainment and the reasonable drinks were all a part of shilling a gambler inside so he could be separated from his money. It was time for me to take a look inside my wallet. Why not? I had forty-seven dollars left. Not too bad, but not enough for a plane to Mexico. Florence may have had some money, but if she did, I didn't know how much. I decided to gamble with what I had anyway.

There were only six players at the nearest crap table. Not many for the size of the table. I got behind the dice and watched the play until it was my turn.

"Next shooter," the house-man intoned, snaking me the dice with his stick. I picked up the dice and laid a ten-spot on the line. Without shaking them I tossed the dice to the other end of the table. Three. I put another ten on the line, threw the dice. Two. Snake Eyes. I put another ten on the line and my last ten on the eleven. The eleven paid thirty-to-one if you hit it with the initial roll. I threw the dice and they bounced wildly when they hit the string in the middle of the table. Eleven. Letting it ride, all of it except the stack on the eleven, I tossed another eleven. I let the line ride. I rolled again. Seven. Again. Seven. Again. Four. I threw the dice five times, came out for a point, made it, then the four. I let it ride and tossed again. Eight. I made a side bet for hard way, and found that I had to wait before I could toss the dice.

There had been six players at the table when I started and I had made the seventh. Now there were more than thirty people crowding the table, all of them trying to get on me before I could make my next roll. I tossed the dice. Eight. About this time I got cautious and I dragged most of the money from the line. I made four more passes and if I hadn't been so careful I would have made some real money. As it was, I walked away from the table with fourteen hundred dollars.

I had another drink at the bar and bought the bartender one. On my way out I dropped five silver dollars into the house-man's shirt pocket as I passed the crap table. Outside, I climbed into a cab and had him drive me to the nearest liquor store. I picked up a fifth of gin and had the driver take me back to the Home Rest Motel. I paid him off, watching him swing in a U through the gravel, and then I entered the cabin. Florence was asleep. I took the roll of bills out of my pocket and riffled them by her ear a few times. She awoke, turned over and faced me.

"Look." I riffled the bills again.

"It looks like a lot of money," she said sleepily.

"Better than fourteen hundred." I grinned at her dazed expression.

"Where'd you get it?" She sat up in bed, wide awake.

"I won it. Shooting craps. Crazy luck, that's all. But it's enough to get away on."

"Will it get us to Mexico City?"

"It should. I don't know. But once and for all, Florence, tell me the truth. Have you really got ten thousand bucks in Mexico City?"

"At the Casa del Oro Hotel." She looked me directly in the eyes and I believed her. There was no other choice. I had to believe her.

"Then let's have a drink and I'll get the ball rolling."

I opened the gin, poured two fingers each into the glasses on the bedside stand, and handed one to Florence.

"Didn't you bring any mix?" she asked, staring distastefully at the straight gin in her glass.

"No. I didn't even think about it. Want some water in it?"

"I'd rather have mix."

"I'll get some Cokes out of the machine by the office."

"No. That's all right, Jake. I can drink it straight."

"It'll only take a minute."

I left the cabin, humming happily, and trotted through the gravel to the office. A red Coke machine was by the door. It took dimes. I looked through my pockets. No change. I had given all of my loose change to the cab driver. I pushed the night bell and Shorty Anderson was at the screen door in nothing flat.

"I need some change for Cokes," I told him.

He was back in a couple of minutes with change for a dollar.

"You get a free newspaper every morning, Mr Smith," he said, a slow smile on his face. "I'd have brought yours down when they came, but I didn't think you'd want to be bothered."

"I just wanted some cokes," I said, dropping a dime into the machine.

"I'll get them for you. It's a trick machine. You gotta kick it after you put the dime in or it won't work. I've told Carl about it a dozen times. But every time he drops a dime in they come right out. Of course, he works for the company and knows more about it than I do." He kicked the machine and a Coke dropped into the receiving slot. "How many you want, Mr Smith?"

"Four ought to do it." I handed him the change and looked at the newspaper he handed me. Nothing in the headlines. I turned the page and there was the item at the top of Page Two. It was headed:

S.F. ARCHITECT FOUND SMOTHERED

The "smothered" fooled me, and if "architect" hadn't been in the subhead, I'd have missed the item altogether. I hadn't smothered Weintraub, I'd clipped him on the jaw . . . Weintraub had been found late Saturday night by Mrs Ronald Watkins, the housekeeper, who had returned home from a movie . . . The housekeeper lived in. That was something else Florence had neglected to tell me.

Mrs Milton Weintraub, who had recently been released from a mental institution on a trial visit, was being sought for questioning. That rocked me. Weintraub had been smothered to death, probably by a pillow, and police suspected foul play. The rest of the short item contained the usual malarkey, most of it supposition.

The only parts that interested me were the facts that Florence was an ex-inmate of a booby hatch and that I hadn't killed Weintraub with my sock to the jaw. I wadded the newspaper and threw it on the ground. As I started toward the cabin, Mr Anderson called me back. "You're forgetting your Cokes," the little man said. I took the four unopened bottles, tucked them under my arm, and returned to the cabin. At the door I paused, made up a lie, and then I went inside.

Florence had fixed her face and a new coral mouth. She was still in bed, but she had put her slip on. I opened one of the Cokes and gave it to her. She poured the contents on top of her gin. We raised our glasses.

"To us," I said. I finished my drink and set the glass down on the bedside table. Florence patted the bed and I sat down beside her. I smiled. She smiled, finished her drink.

"Well, baby," I said. "We're really in luck."

"I'll say. Fourteen hundred dollars . . . "

"And now for Mexico. Know where San Berdoo is?"

"Of course."

"Well, I've got an old friend there, a pilot I knew in the army, and he owns his own plane. He owes me a favor and he'll take us to Mexico with no questions asked."

"Isn't it dangerous to go back to California?"

"For us, baby, it's dangerous anywhere. The sooner we get out of the country, the better."

"Don't you think we'd better wait until tonight?"

"The alarm might be out by then. We'd better leave right now."

"I wish you'd mentioned San Berdoo last night, before we drove—"

"If we hadn't come to Vegas, we wouldn't have been married, and I wouldn't have won fourteen hundred dollars. Now get dressed, and let's get the hell out of here." I smiled and it hurt my lips. I felt more like choking her.

While Florence dressed I had another drink. I sipped it slowly, thinking things out. The first thing to do was to get her back to California. And once we crossed the line I could turn in at the nearest police station. Hell, I had a fighting chance now. I had known already that Florence was a little screwy, but I hadn't suspected that she was actually crazy. Not until I read the newspaper item. That gave me my chance. Florence must have killed Weintraub, not me. She must have smothered him while I was in the kitchen getting the pan of water to bring him around. No point in trying to run away now. I had enough of a chance to get off the hook and I was taking it. And to top it off, I had a nice little wad of dough. Enough for a fair, if not a good, lawyer.

"I'm ready, Jake," Florence said. "I sure hate to leave that bed," she added wistfully.

"We'll have all the time in the world in Mexico." I picked up the over-nighter, opened the door and shooed her outside. "Want me to drive for awhile, Florence?"

"No. I'm rested now. I'd better drive."

In a few minutes we had left The Strip behind and we were on the open highway. By the time we hit the mile-long stretch of dips she was doing better than eighty miles an hour. We passed a billboard and a moment later a siren screamed behind us. I looked out the rear window. A state patrolman was trailing us on a motorcycle and gradually closing the gap.

"Well, baby," I said angrily, "we won't get to California after all. But women nuts enough to smother their husbands are easily extradited!"

The look on her face made me laugh.

CHAPTER
13

I didn't enjoy my laughter very long.

Florence's face, naturally pale, lost what little color it had. She wet her lips with the tip of her pink tongue. Her eyes lost their luster and turned a dull, dusty purplish color. Viciously, she jammed the accelerator to the floor. The Buick leaped forward with a burst of speed I hadn't suspected it possessed. I think, now, that Florence might have got away from the motorcycle, if it hadn't been for the dips. And the S curve that appeared for no good reason except the slight rise of ground . . . The Buick squealed around the first curve on two wheels, but Florence was going much too fast to make the second curve. As she spun the wheel madly for the second half of the S we hit the dip and the car bounded the other way into the desert. It ploughed through loose sand for about forty yards, going slower and slower, and then like a tired elephant, it turned over and came to rest at a sharp angle against a low, loose pile of sand. I tried to open the door, but slid down the sloping seat into Florence. On my next attempt I held the handle down tightly and heaved hard against it with my shoulder. It flew open. I climbed out, dropped to the ground, and noticed that the right front wheel was still spinning.

"Are you all right, Florence?" I stood on the ground, reaching up to hold the door open with my left hand. Florence's head appeared, her left hand clutched the seat, and she was part way out. She looked at me as though I was an odd, over-large insect pinned wiggling to a board. Her right hand cleared the top of the seat, and before I noticed the tiny pistol in her hand she fired quickly, without aiming. The bullet spanged into the metal edge of the door. I released the door in a hurry and started running across the desert toward the highway. The patrolman had stopped his motorcycle well past the second curve and was puffing on foot through the loose sand, a small gray first-aid kit clutched in his hand. He was a big man, built like a lamp, with narrow shoulders, an overhanging paunch, and an enormous rear end. I signaled to him.

"Follow me!" I shouted.

He halted, planted his feet, and looked first at me, then at the car. From the way he ducked, a bullet must have narrowly missed him. I looked over my shoulder and saw Florence drop to the ground and line up her pistol for another shot at the patrolman. He saw the pistol and started running again. Both of us reached the highway at the same time.

"Let's get behind the billboard," I said, pointing across the road. We ran across the highway and got behind the billboard, and lay down next to each other where we could look through the green lattice-work at the bottom of the sign. The patrolman puffed and panted, his red face dripping with perspiration.

"What's the matter with her?" he asked between gasps. "Is she crazy or something?"

"You can say that again," I answered. "It's Florence Weintraub."

"Is that supposed to explain something?"

"I'm Jacob C. Blake."

"Oh. We're looking for you."

A bullet went through the sign about three feet above our heads.

"She's a little high," I said.

"She's trying to kill us!"

"Now you've got the general idea."

The patrolman was very frightened. His body quivered with fear. His large red hands trembled like a man with dengue fever. I felt contempt for the overgrown clown. I was afraid too, but at least I could control it.

"Listen, blubberbutt," I said. "That's Florence Weintraub over there. She's wanted in San Francisco for murdering her husband. Go and get her!"

"I'm not going no place!" He pushed his face into the sand and covered his head with his hands. I peeked through the crisscrossed laths, trying to see where Florence was hiding. All I could see was a lot of pink dirt, cacti, and three widely spaced Joshua trees.

It was up to me.

I would have preferred to have the patrolman shoot her. I liked Florence all right, even if she was nutty. But to remain behind the billboard would have been sheer stupidity. If this had been combat, and the patrolman had been in my squad, and if I'd told him to move out and he hadn't, I would have shot him then and there. But it wasn't combat . . . and he wasn't in my squad.

"Give me your gun," I ordered.

He reached down to his hip, unfastened the leather strap that held his pistol in its holster, and gave me the weapon.

"What are you going to do?" There was a thin ring of white around his mouth. His forehead and eyebrows were covered with sand from pressing his face against the ground. "I'm going to kill her. She's wanted for murder. it's legal, isn't it, to kill a murderer?"

"Suppose you don't? I'll be here without my gun, and she'll be over here after me . . . and . . . and . . . "

"Don't cry, Sonny Boy." I was amazed at his abject fear. How do they train these guys, anyway? Surely there is more to law and order than passing out tickets for speeding. I could hardly keep the disgust out of my voice.

"Now listen to me," I said. "I'm going to crawl down the ditch there . . . to the dip. I'll cross the highway through the dip and she won't be able to see me. When I get close enough for a shot at her, it'll all be over. Meantime, to cover for me, you start talking to her to hold her attention. It's very simple. Hold and flank. Do you understand?"

"What do I say to her?" His lower lip trembled.

"Anything. Tell her to give up, throw her pistol into the road, things like that."

"What if she rushes me? And I don't have any—"

"All the better. I'll be behind her by that time and I can get a better shot."

He nodded, peered anxiously through the lattice-work, and worked his mouth several times.

"Give up, Mrs Weintraub!" he shouted. His voice was squeaky, a full octave higher than his speaking voice.

I crawled along the length of the sign toward the ditch. I squirmed along on my belly. A baby creeps and a snake crawls. I crawled, my head low to the ground. In a way, it was like being on a patrol. I was excited. There was a taste of copper in my mouth and every sense was alive and tingling. This is why there is war. Men like this highly exalted feeling. Hunting animals is a poor substitute for the real thing. The only time a man is really alive is when he is close to death. I reached the ditch and rolled into it sideways, being careful with my feet so they wouldn't raise above the level of the rest of my body. I made better time in the ditch; it was almost three feet deep.

"Throw your pistol out in the road, Mrs Weintraub!" It was the patrolman again, with his high, womanish voice.

"The hell with you!" Florence answered for the first time. I grinned. "Send that sneaky, son-of-a-bitch out here!" Florence screamed. "After I kill him you can have this goddam pistol!"

Good. He had her talking, had her attention. I reached the dip and I hesitated. The dip gave me a bad moment. It wasn't as deep as I had thought it was. If a level was stretched across it, the bottom wouldn't have been more than a foot-and-a-half deep. But a car speeding down the highway wouldn't be able to see me crawling across it, because of the first half of the S curve. I had to take the chance. Both ways. If Florence spotted me, and I didn't know where she was, she'd pump four or five of those little .25 caliber bullets into me. Well . . .

I crawled across slowly, quietly, holding my speed down with all of the patience I could muster. If I made any noise, I'd be two hundred pounds of exposed body stretched flat on the asphalt highway. As I reached the other side of the road, a swiftly moving Merc convertible swung around the first curve, made the other one, and roared down the road. Lying flat on the ground I couldn't see the driver. The unseen driver must have seen the patrolman's motorcycle, but that was no reason for him to stop. I lay there quietly until the sound of the powerful engine faded out of range.

The butt of the heavy .45 automatic was clutched tightly in my hand. I hadn't checked the weapon to see whether there was a round in the chamber or not. Silently, I cursed myself.

"Give up, Mrs Weintraub! You haven't got a chance!" the patrolman shouted.

Florence didn't answer.

I gripped the slide with my left hand and slid it back a quarter of an inch at a time until it was back all the way. I let it forward just as slowly and felt the first round leave the magazine and slide into the chamber. The safety was off. The hammer was at full cock. I inched my way across the sand to a small clump of cactus blooming with bristly red fruit. I got to my knees.

Florence was in plain sight, less than twenty yards away. She was crouched behind a Joshua tree like a movie cowboy. Her knees were bent, and she held her arm straight out in front of her, the pistol in her hand. Her eyes and head jerked back and forth warily, as she tried to watch both ends of the billboard at the same time. It was ludicrous, and at the same time, it was touching . . . in a way. I got to my feet slowly, taking my time. She didn't dream that I was to her left and slightly behind her.

I put my left hand in my hip pocket, did a half-right face, and aimed carefully. Over the V-sight, my bull's eye was her mop of dark, tousled hair. I squeezed the trigger. She hit the ground hard. The force of the heavy slug was like being hit with a locomotive. Her small, pearl-handled pistol flew through the air and fell to the ground.

I trudged through the sand and looked down at her body. The lower half of her jaw was gone. Her jaw had deflected the bullet and it had pierced the roof of her mouth and entered her brain. Her upper teeth were all exposed in a cruel grin. Her eyes were the color of dusty blackberries without the slightest flicker of life. There was a run in her left stocking and the shoe was lost somewhere, probably back in the Buick. Tiny, black flies appeared from somewhere and bounced up and down on her bloody face like a handful of BBs dropped on the sidewalk. Overhead, a buzzard hung like a black kite in the sky. It banked tightly and then, head to the meager wind, anchored itself and waited.

I removed the magazine, jerked the slide back, and ejected the new round. I pulled the trigger of the empty pistol, replaced the magazine.

"All right, officer!" I called across the road. "You can come out now! The game is over."

Charles Willeford

CHAPTER

14

The patrolman came out from behind the billboard and nervously crossed the road. I stood beside the Joshua tree, dangling his pistol by the trigger guard from my right forefinger.

"Is she dead?" he asked anxiously.

"Take a look." I jerked my head and handed him the pistol. I walked over to a crumble of boulders and sat down. I lit a cigarette and watched the patrolman with amusement. He took one hard look at Florence, stumbled away from her, dropped to his knees and tossed his lunch on the sand. He kept retching for quite a spell.

That's the way it is with guys who haven't seen it before. Violent death is a lot different from any other kind. Of course, he'd seen mangled bodies before. Every highway patrolman has. There are a great many wrecks on the highway in the course of a year. A murder, though, is something else again. It sort of adds to the shock. I didn't feel sorry for the cop. His should have been the life that was risked going after Florence. Not mine. The hell with him.

He got off his knees, and carefully averting his eyes from the body, sat down on a boulder next to me. I gave him a cigarette and a light. He looked a little better. The redness was back in his weather-beaten face. He took three deep drags on his cigarette in succession, inhaling with calm deliberation.

"All right, Blake," he said, nice and friendly, "what's the story on this?"

"You don't know?"

"No, but I want it straight. It's between you and me."

"Okay. It's simple, and I'm clean. Without going into detail, I was at her house in San Francisco when her husband came in. We had a little argument and I slugged him. When I went into the kitchen to get some water to bring him out of it, she smothered him with a pillow. You can check this easy enough. It's in the Vegas paper."

"What else?"

"She told me I killed him. Well, not exactly. I assumed I'd killed him. I didn't know she had smothered him while I was out of the room. Anyway, we left town, and drove down to Vegas. I read the paper this morning and she didn't. I told her we could get a plane in San Berdoo for Mexico, and we were driving back to California when you got on our tail. I was going to turn in just as soon as I hit a California police station.

"Is that straight?"

"That's straight."

"What do you want to do now?"

"Get cleared."

"What about her?"

"She's dead."

"I know that. But . . . " His hand holding the cigarette was shaking. "Do you think it would help your case when it came out that you shot her?"

I thought this over.

"No."

"Well, then . . . " His face turned a brighter shade of red. "Would you object to saying that it was me that shot her?" There was nothing ingratiating about the tone of his voice. He was direct about it. I have to give him that much credit.

"That would be a favor to me, for Christ's sake," I said.

"It would be a bigger favor to me."

I saw his point. It wouldn't look good for a uniformed officer of the law to hide behind a billboard while a civilian took his gun and shot an armed woman. And it would be to his credit if he shot a wanted murderer . . .

"You tell it anyway you want to, Officer. From now on I'm a clam, anyway. And I won't make any changes in your story."

"I appreciate this, Blake." We shook hands on it.

From then on, events moved fast. The patrolman called in on his radio, and in a few minutes a patrol car pulled up and took me back to the Vegas jail. The patrolman stayed with the body to await the sheriff, coroner and so on. I was glad to reach the air-conditioned jail and get away from the scene.

At the desk I played it innocent. I emptied my pockets and put my stuff on the desk, first counting my money, and making certain that the correct amount was written on the brown manila envelope before it was sealed.

"What's my connection with this Weintraub case, Sergeant?" I asked, smiling. "I don't get it."

"Neither do I. Nothing, as far as I know. But we'll find out when San Francisco tells us. Your name wasn't mentioned on the Weintraub all-points."

"Then what are you holding me for?"

"We've got a separate all-points on you." He grunted.

"Let me see . . . " He dug through the stack of correspondence on the desk. "Here it is," he said, holding up a yellow flimsy. I had to wait while he put his glasses on. "'Wanted: Jacob C. Blake, Private Investigator.' You a private investigator?"

"Yes, sir."

"Well, what do you know about that! I've never met one before. 'Description: Height, five-ten.' You look taller than that."

"That's because I stand straight."

"I see. 'Weight: two hundred pounds. Eyes: blue. Hair: blond. Complexion: ruddy.' You don't have a ruddy complexion."

"They always say ruddy when the hair's blond," I said impatiently.

"You're right about that. I do myself. 'Identifying marks: three-inch scar, left buttock. One-inch scar, right calf. Eight-inch scar, chest, diagonal from left shoulder to left nipple. Missing:

little finger, left hand. Tattoo: scroll and red roses, left forearm. Inscription: "Mother."' Let me see that."

I removed my jacket, rolled up my sleeve and showed him the tattoo.

"How come it's so faded?" he asked curiously.

"I tried to have it taken off. Couldn't be done."

"I could have told you that. Once they're on there, that's it. Here it is: 'Wanted by San Francisco police for the murder of Jefferson Davis.'"

"Read that last sentence again, Sergeant."

"'Wanted by San Francisco police for the murder of Jefferson Davis.' That's all it says, Blake."

"Thanks," I said.

They put me in a cell. I asked no more questions and I said nothing more about anything. I did make a statement about the death of Florence, adding an ironical last paragraph to the effect that Patrolman Burgess was one of the bravest men I'd ever seen in his fearless attack against the armed woman. But as to myself being on the scene, I said nothing. The Jefferson Davis deal was mystifying, and I believed the wisest course was to keep my mouth shut. Not that it made any difference in the long run . . .

• • •

The jail was all right. They let me spend my money and I had decent meals brought in from a restaurant down the street. I bought magazines to read, and the air-conditioning made me forget the desert heat. I passed three days in bodily comfort, at least.

On the third day, the sheriff brought a waiver for extradition to California to my cell. I signed it. Why not? They could get me back anyway. That afternoon I was leafing through a *Life* when the turnkey said something to me through the bars. I looked up.

"What's that?" I asked him.

"You've got some visitors. Want to see 'em?"

"Sure. Who are they?"

"San Francisco detective; a man named Allen, and his daughter."

It was Lieutenant Stanley Pulaski, Barbara Ann Allen, and the man was Barbara's father, not Freddy. Mr. Allen was prosperous-looking, with a rosy complexion and four inches of side hair combed over a bald spot. He wore a yellow linen suit. Pulaski looked miserably hot in a heavy, blue serge suit. All three of them stared at me curiously for a minute or so, and then Pulaski put his big hand gently on Barbara's arm.

"Is this the man, Barbara?" Pulaski asked her.

"Yes, sir," she said.

"Are you sure, Bobby?" her father asked.

"I'm positive," she replied.

Pulaski grinned, and slowly removed a cigar from its glass tube. He cut the end off with a knife and lit it carefully.

"I don't get it," I said. "Somebody's up to something and I'd like to know the score. The last time I saw Mr Davis, he was very much alive. I didn't even know he was dead until the desk sergeant told me I was wanted in connection with his death."

Mr Allen laughed without humor and nudged Barbara Ann. She compressed her lips and glared at me.

"Oh, you dirty, dirty, dirty liar, you! I was in the lobby when you left the hotel! I saw you leave the hotel with the bundle under your arm!"

"Suppose you tell me how he was killed then? It's a mystery to me."

"You'd do better, Blake," Mr Allen said, "to save this innocent act for the courtroom. But it won't do you any good. My son, Freddy, saw you leave Davis' room right after you cut his throat. You might have thought that the vicious beating you gave my boy was enough to keep him quiet, but you were wrong! We Allens are made of sterner stuff than that. Freddy will be avenged for that beating—I swear, I swear!" His voice broke and tears rolled down his cheeks. He took a silk handkerchief out of his hip pocket and blew his nose.

"Please, Daddy," Barbara Ann said, "let's go. This is the man . . . that's all you wanted to know."

They walked down the corridor, leaving Pulaski behind. Pulaski had a smug, self-satisfied look on his dew-lapped face. Sweat rolled down my back and I felt cold all over, with that strange feeling that a heated body feels under air-conditioning.

"Listen, Pulaski I said desperately, "I didn't have anything to do with this. I swear it! I'll admit I worked Freddy over a little bit, but—"

"I guess you did, Blake. He's still in the hospital."

"The reason I hit Freddy a few times was because he hit me first. He ruined my suit with a damned fire extinguisher.

"What did you do with the suit, Blake?"

"I put it on the bumper of a passing car."

"Because it had blood on it?"

"No, there wasn't any blood on the suit. It had that acid and soda mixture all over it, from the fire extinguisher."

"Do you expect me to believe that?"

"Yes!"

"Well, I don't. You're going to the gas chamber, Blake. You're guilty and for once you can't claim a frame. Freddy even found your knife that you left behind, and he turned it in . . . "

"That's his knife!"

"I suppose you claim that Freddy killed Davis?" Pulaski snorted.

"It must have been him. I didn't do it!"

"The desk clerk said that you and Davis were talking together in the lobby . . . "

"What of it? I just met the man and we were talking about his pictures—!"

"I'm going to tell you something, Blake. I don't like you and I never have, but if I thought you were innocent I'd go to bat for you. You're as guilty as hell. We've got the knife you used; we know that you got rid of the clothes you wore because they had blood on them, and we've got a sworn statement from Freddy Allen that you beat him up in an attempt to make him keep his mouth shut. To top that, the hotel switchboard has a record of a call that Davis made to you in your room. We don't need any more, Blake. And Barbara Ann, who was waiting for her brother, saw you cross the lobby with a bundle under your arm . . . "

"That doesn't prove anything."

"The jury'll decide that."

"How about a deal, Lieutenant? I'll admit I was mixed up in the Weintraub case, and that I hit—"

"No soap. We're holding that up, just in case. Your prints were all over the room, but we won't need that case. The one we've got is better. I'll see you in court, Blake."

He turned heavily and clomped down the corridor.

There isn't any use to tell about the trial. It was in all the papers. The only defense I had was the fact that I was a good soldier during the war. My lawyer passed my medals around the jury box, and they were closely examined.

They didn't help a bit.

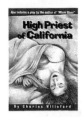

RE/Search #13: Angry Women

16 cutting-edge performance artists discuss critical questions such as: How can you have a revolutionary feminism that encompasses wild sex, humor, beauty and spirituality *plus* radical politics? How can you have a powerful movement for social change that's *inclusionary*—not exclusionary? A wide range of topics—from menstruation, masturbation, vibrators, S&M & spanking to racism, failed Utopias and the death of the Sixties—are discussed passionately. Armed with total contempt for dogma, stereotype and cliche, these creative visionaries probe deep into our social foundation of taboos, beliefs and totalitarian linguistic contradictions from whence spring (as well as thwart) our theories, imaginings, behavior and dreams. 8½x11", 240 pp, 135 photos & illustrations. **$18.99**

RE/Search People Series, Volume I: Bob Flanagan, Super-Masochist

Bob Flanagan, born in 1952 in New York City, grew up with Cystic Fibrosis (a genetically inherited, nearly-always fatal disease) and has lived longer than any other person with CF. The physical pain of his childhood suffering was principally alleviated by masturbation and sexual experimentation, wherein pain and pleasure became inextricably linked, resulting in his lifelong practice of extreme masochism.

In deeply confessional interviews, Bob details his sexual practices and his extraordinary relationship with long-term partner and Mistress, photographer Sheree Rose. He tells how frequent near-death encounters modified his concepts of gratification and abstinence, reward and punishment, and intensified his masochistic drive. Through his insider's perspective on the Sado-Masochistic community, we learn firsthand about branding, piercing, whipping, bondage and endurance trials. Includes photographs by L.A. artist Sheree Rose. 8½ x 11", 128 pp, 125 photos & illustrations. **$14.99**

RE/Search #12: Modern Primitives

An eye-opening, startling investigation of the undercover world of body modifications: tattooing, piercing and scarification. Amazing, explicit photos! *Fakir Musafar* (55-yr-old Silicon Valley ad executive who, since age 14, has practiced every body modification known to man); *Genesis & Paula P-Orridge* describing numerous ritual scarifications and personal, symbolic tattoos; *Ed Hardy* (editor of *Tattootime* and creator of over 10,000 tattoos); *Capt. Don Leslie* (sword-swallower); *Jim Ward* (editor, *Piercing Fans International*); *Anton LaVey* (founder of the Church of Satan); *Lyle Tuttle* (talking about getting tattooed in Samoa); *Raelyn Gallina* (women's piercer) & others talk about body practices that develop identity, sexual sensation and philosophic awareness. This issue spans the spectrum from S&M pain to New Age ecstasy. 22 interviews, 2 essays (including a treatise on Mayan body piercing based on recent findings), quotations, sources/bibliography & index. 8½ x 11", 216 pp, 279 photos & illustrations. **$17.99**

RE/Search #11: Pranks!

A prank is a "trick, a mischievous act, a ludicrous act." Although not regarded as poetic or artistic acts, pranks constitute an art form and genre in themselves. Here pranksters such as Timothy Leary, Abbie Hoffman, Paul Krassner, Mark Pauline, Monte Cazazza, Jello Biafra, Earth First!, Joe Coleman, Karen Finley, Frank Discussion, John Waters and Henry Rollins challenge the sovereign authority of words, images & behavioral convention. Some tales are bizarre, as when Boyd Rice presented the First Lady with a skinned sheep's head on a platter. This iconoclastic compendium will dazzle and delight all lovers of humor, satire and irony. 8½ x 11", 244 pp, 164 photos & illustrations. **$17.99**

RE/Search #10: Incredibly Strange Films

A guide to important territory neglected by the film criticism establishment, spotlighting unhailed directors—*Herschell Gordon Lewis, Russ Meyer, Larry Cohen, Ray Dennis Steckler, Ted V. Mikels, Doris Wishman* and others—who have been critically consigned to the ghettos of gore and sexploitation films. In-depth interviews focus on philosophy, while anecdotes entertain as well as illuminate theory. 13 interviews, numerous essays, A-Z of film personalities, "Favorite Films" list, quotations, bibliography, filmography, film synopses, & index. 8½ x 11", 228 pp. 157 photos & illustrations. **$17.99**

RE/Search #8/9: J.G. Ballard

A comprehensive special on this supremely relevant writer, now famous for *Empire of the Sun* and *Day of Creation*. W.S. Burroughs described Ballard's novel *Love & Napalm: Export U.S.A.* (1972) as "profound and disquieting...This book stirs sexual depths untouched by the hardest-core illustrated porn." 3 interviews, biography by David Pringle, fiction and non-fiction excerpts, essays, quotations, bibliography, sources, & index. 8½ x 11", 176 pp. 76 photos & illustrations by Ana Barrado, Ken Werner, Ed Ruscha, and others. **$14.99**

The Atrocity Exhibition by J.G. Ballard

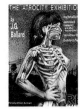

A large-format, illustrated edition of this long out-of-print classic, widely regarded as Ballard's finest, most complex work. Withdrawn by E.P. Dutton after having been shredded by Doubleday, this outrageous work was finally printed in a small edition by Grove before lapsing out of print 15 years ago. With 4 additional fiction pieces, extensive annotations (a book in themselves), disturbing photographs by Ana Barrado and dazzling, anatomically explicit medical illustrations by Phoebe Gloeckner. 8½ x 11", 140pp. **$13.99**